THEO slugg
in dead trouble

Simon Goswell

■SCHOLASTIC

Scholastic Children's Books,
Commonwealth House, 1–19 New Oxford Street,
London, WC1A 1NU, UK
A division of Scholastic Ltd
London ~ New York ~ Toronto ~ Sydney ~ Auckland
Mexico City ~ New Delhi ~ Hong Kong

First published in the UK by Scholastic Ltd, 2004

ISBN 0 439 97765 7

Printed and bound by Nørhaven Paperback A/S, Denmark

10 9 8 7 6 5 4 3 2 1

A WARNING

Have you ever seen a ghost? Perhaps not. But that doesn't mean they're not about. That slight tickly feeling at the back of your neck right now might be a ghost. Think about it. That could be their cold breath on your neck as they read this book over your shoulder. Someone long dead might be standing by your elbow. Just because you can't see them doesn't mean that they're not there. They might be waiting until exactly the right moment to jump out and give you a fright.

Not that you *would* be frightened, of course. Ghosts can't actually *do* anything, can they? They're nothing really. Just wispy things that float about like lost sheets going "wooo, wooo".

Or are they? Maybe ghosts can do things, when they feel like it. What do you think?

But whatever you think about ghosts, here are a few words of warning: it's probably a good idea to treat the dead with respect. It's not really worth the risk, is it? If you don't, and something nasty happens, don't say I didn't warn you. . .

The Slugg family lived in a small flat at the top of a building called Vanilla Villas in the charming seaside town of Bunting-on-Sea. Mr and Mrs Slugg had 14 daughters who were all under the age of eight* and were all very musical and talented. They also had one son, Theo, who was 12 and who liked doing nothing in particular.

The flat was rather cramped and noisy with all those musical sisters so Theo had moved into the lift. He'd made his corner quite comfortable. He had a bed, a small television, a few books, a couple of

* In case you're wondering: two lots of triplets and four sets of twins. (And don't worry, there won't be any more of these silly footnotes to distract you when you're trying to read the book. Now get back to the story!)

pictures and a curtain made from an old tartan rug. Theo soon got used to people going up and down and he was quite happy until one night his grandma got into the lift. This wouldn't have been odd except for the fact that she had been dead for three months.

"G-g-g-grandma!" gasped Theo, shaking.

Theo was scared. And not just because it was the first time he had seen a ghost. That was bad enough. But Theo had never been very fond of his grandma. She'd always bossed him around and thought him lazy and selfish. It has to be said that when she was being buried and her coffin lowered into the ground, Theo had looked on more with enthusiasm than sadness. So you can imagine how he felt when she turned up in his bedroom.

"Get out of bed, you little squit," said Grandma. "And close that mouth of yours before a bluebottle flies in." She prodded Theo with her walking stick.

"B-b-b-but Grandma, y-you're DEAD!" cried Theo, trying to avoid the stick. Surely this wasn't really happening? Surely he was dreaming? His grandma looked so real, not at all like he'd expect a ghost to look. There she was, as bright as day in the darkness of the lift, a slight hazy blue glow around her.

"Being dead is not going to stop me. Nothing is

8

going to stop me," said Grandma. "There are things to be done."

I need hardly tell you that Theo's grandma had always been one of those people who "did things". In her youth she had disguised herself as a man and joined the Navy. After a long and successful career as a boiler-room stoker she had finally married a librarian called Martin and settled down to have a family. But that hadn't stopped her doing things.

"Now get out of bed," barked Grandma again, "I want you to meet some dead people."

More dead people! Theo shrank back beneath the bedclothes.

"Grandma, I've g-got to sleep. I've g-got school tomorrow," he said.

"Rubbish, you lying little toad!" said Grandma. "You've no school tomorrow because it's the holidays. I might be dead but I'm not stupid. Now get up and come and say hello to your relatives."

"I'm not coming. I'm staying here. In bed," said Theo, who had at last found some courage. "I'm going to sleep, Grandma. Go away, please." This was a brave thing to say but, then again, perhaps a little bit foolish. You may have observed that bravery and stupidity are often not far apart.

"You stubborn little sprat," said Grandma. "Not coming, eh? We'll see about that."

She gave the bedclothes one last whack with her walking stick, then turned around and stormed off through the closed lift doors.

"We'll see about that" was one of Grandma's many favourite sayings. And as you probably know, when someone says "we'll see about that", it generally means that there's trouble on the way.

At some point in the middle of the night, Theo woke up. Something cold and slimy was crawling up his leg. He leapt out of bed and peered down.

The slimy thing was a warty green toad.

"Urghh! Get off. Get off!"

Theo shook his leg. After a lot of shaking, the toad fell on to the floor. It then disappeared *through* the floor. If Theo had been a little more awake, this might have made him suspicious. As it was, he was too sleepy to notice. He climbed back into bed, pulled the duvet around him and went back to sleep.

A couple of hours later, Theo woke again. This time his bed was full of toads and they were wriggling all over him. He leapt out of bed, tugging furiously at his pyjamas. Where had they come from? The horrible, slimy things were everywhere.

"Urghh! Ahhh!"

He had to get rid of them!

He grabbed a book and started scooping the toads into his rubbish bin. He put another book on top to stop them getting out.

But it wasn't any good. The toads crawled straight back out through the sides of the bin. Whatever Theo tried, nothing would keep them in.

"Argh!" muttered Theo, crossly. "Phantom toads! I should have known. Grandma's behind this!" Now that he was fully awake he could see that the toads all had a very slight bluish glow, just like his grandma's ghost.

For a moment he stood wondering what to do next, with the toads crawling all over everywhere. Then Theo saw that the toads were forming themselves into several neat lines. At first he thought that they were getting ready to rush him. But one toad, somewhat larger than the rest, waddled to the front and bowed. It turned to face the others and waved at them a couple of times to get their attention. Theo watched, puzzled and amazed.

"One, two, three, four," croaked the toad. And the toads began to sing:

"The cherry blossom on the trees,
Is swinging gaily in the breeze,
And little birdies sweetly sing
Of happy days and—"

"Oh, I get it!" cried Theo. "Stop! Stop it! I get the idea. Grandma knows I can't stand that stupid song. It's my sisters' favourite. They love it so much they sing it the whole time. It makes me sick. Yuck!"

"But she said that you'd love to hear it," said the toads. "It's our favourite too." And they began again. *"The cherry blossom on—"*

"No, stop!" cried Theo. "Grandma was having you on. I hate it."

The toads shuffled about awkwardly.

"I think you'd better go away. Tell Grandma her little plan didn't work."

"So you won't come and meet your relatives?" asked the large toad.

"No," said Theo.

The toads looked miserable. They limped off to the side of the lift and began to disappear through the wall.

"Press button B if you change your mind," mumbled the large toad, a tear glistening in the corner of his eye.

Theo sat down on his bed feeling very cross. His grandmother had always been a nagging old bat. *Do this, do that!* Never what *he* wanted to do. When she had died he'd thought he could be himself at last. But now she was at it again. And perhaps it was worse than when she'd been alive. Now she was a ghost she could appear whenever she felt like it! He'd have no life of his own. Theo shuddered at the thought.

But what could he do to stop her? His grandma hadn't usually taken no for an answer. When she told someone to do something they did it, or else life became very unpleasant.

Theo realized that he would have to find out what she was up to. He'd have to meet Grandma and his other relatives. Perhaps, if he did what she wanted, then she'd leave him alone. He'd have to try it. It was the only way. He'd have to press button B.

Having made up his mind, Theo dressed quickly and walked over to the lift buttons. He stared at the one marked B. The basement. Surely his ghostly relatives weren't all in the basement? There were only two rooms. One was a storeroom where the janitor, Mr Windrush, kept his cleaning things. And the other had a large washing machine that nobody ever used. Theo shrugged and gave the button a firm push.

The lift started travelling downwards. The indicator above the door lit up as it passed the floors: 3 . . . 2 . . . 1 . . . G (for the ground floor) and then B. The B lit up and then went out again. The lift didn't stop. It went on going down.

It's an odd thing about lifts but you really have no idea where you are when you're inside. There are only those little lights to tell you. And when you stop, for all you know the doors could open anywhere. Suppose for a moment, that instead of the building where you started, the doors opened on Arizona, or Antarctica or Abergavenny. It would be surprising but, when you're in a lift, it doesn't seem impossible. Theo was wondering about this as the lift went on down.

There was a jolt and the lift stopped.

For a second, nothing happened. Then the doors slid open slowly and Theo peered out. I can't describe what Theo saw, for the simple reason that there was nothing to see. Absolutely nothing at all.

"Ah, I thought the toads might do the trick," said a voice.

Theo peered into the darkness. He knew it was his grandma that had spoken but he couldn't see her. Then she appeared, just as if she'd been switched on like a light. She was standing alone, leaning on her walking stick. There wasn't anything else that Theo could see, no ground or sky, just his grandma's ghost glowing in the dark, the hazy blue around her much brighter than it had been in the lift.

"They didn't. I changed my mind," said Theo, shivering. It was icy cold.

"Really?" said Grandma. "Then you're not as much of an idiot as I thought. Welcome to Deadland. Come and meet some of your relatives."

Theo hesitated.

"It's all right. You won't fall. There's nowhere to fall to."

Theo put one foot out of the lift, testing the nothingness. To his surprise, his foot didn't sink. Where the ground should be was solid. He tried the other foot. Then he took a few steps. It was an odd sensation, walking on nothing, his footsteps making no sound.

He joined his grandmother. They walked together, Grandma hobbling along, leading the way, although Theo couldn't see how she could tell where they were going. He glanced back towards the lift. It was still there, the light shining inside. Otherwise all around him was nothingness. He walked slowly, afraid he'd fall or bump into something he couldn't see.

"It's not far," said his grandma.

Then Theo saw that a short distance away there was a large gathering of ghosts. They were all like his grandma, with the same hazy blue glow around them. Theo also noted with alarm that they were mostly ugly. Were they really his relatives?

"This is Theo, my grandson," said Grandma, as they approached.

The dead people pressed around Theo. They

peered at him closely and plucked at his clothing.

"Ooooh, a live person. I haven't seen one of them for a very long time," said an old woman in a dismal bonnet and a long dress.

"Lovely 'n' pink, isn't he?" said a man in a dusty three-cornered hat.

"We've been *dying* to meet you. Ha, ha, ha, ha!" said another man, who laughed so much his head fell off.

"He's so *warm*," said the woman in the long dress, stroking Theo's cheek. He shrank away from her chilly touch.

"All right, all right, that's enough," said Grandma. "I didn't get him here so you lot could gawp. Down to business. Where's Pete?"

The crowd fell back. They stopped chattering. A man in a checked suit shuffled forward. He had bulgy eyes and two large front teeth that stuck out over his lower lip. He smiled apologetically at Theo.

"Theo, this is Pete Pilkington," said Grandma, "famous as Fast Feet Pete, the wonder tap-dancer of Bunting."

Theo, who was beginning to get suspicious, stared at Pete. He'd never heard of him or his famous tap-dancing.

"He's your great-great-great uncle on your father's mother's side," added Grandma.

This meant nothing to Theo.

"Pleased to meet you," said Pete. He came forward to shake Theo's hand but the moment his hands were out of his pockets Pete's legs parted company with the top half of his body and started wandering off on their own.

"Aw, sorry," said Pete. "That's always happening. It's so embarrassing. You see, I'm missing a bit in me middle. I'm a bottom-less ghost."

"What?" said Theo.

"That Jellicon man has got his pelvis," said Grandma.

"It's true," said Pete, nodding sadly. "You know Jellicon?"

"Who doesn't?" said Theo.

Josiah Jellicon was the owner of Jellicon Comestibles, a local firm which made jams, spreads, chutneys and pickles. The factory was the biggest in the area and lots of local people worked there. Jellicon had a reputation for being a bit mean with the wages but people didn't complain. There weren't that many jobs around. And Jellicon was a powerful man who might have made their lives unpleasant.

"Well, when I died, I drowned," went on Pete, who had got his legs back and was keeping his hands firmly in his pockets. "I went down on HMS *Reginald* in 1941. And me bones has lain undisturbed on the ocean floor ever since. That's until a little while ago, when one of them seaweed collectors Jellicon uses dredged up the bone of me bottom. And now the man's got it stuck on his desk as a paperweight!"

There were murmurings of disgust from the other ghosts. One of them actually spat.

"It's true, Theo," said Grandma.

Theo had heard about the seaweed collectors. There was a rumour that Jellicon's jams weren't made with real fruit, that seaweed was used instead, but Theo's dad, who operated a raspberry pip machine in the factory, said he was sure it wasn't true.

"He's cursed because of it, Theo!" said Pete. "You shouldn't take the bones of the dead. Everybody knows that!"

Theo thought that Mr Jellicon didn't act as though he was cursed. He was a rich man and seemed to do exactly what he wanted.

"So I can't dance as I used to, all because of Jellicon," said Pete.

"So you see, Theo—" began Grandma, but she was interrupted by the woman in the long dress.

"A toast!" cried the woman. "A toast!"

"A ghostly toastly!" chimed in the man in the three-cornered hat.

A young man with a runny nose handed round glasses full of a dark brown liquid.

"Would you like some?" Pete asked. "It's gravy."

"Gravy? Yuck!" said Theo. "No thanks."

They all raised their glasses. "To Theo, who's going to help us!" cried the woman in the long dress.

"What?" said Theo. "*WHAT DID YOU SAY?*"

"You're going to help," said Grandma. "Help get back Pete's bone."

"No, I'm not!" said Theo. "What do you expect me to do? Walk into Jellicon's office and say: 'Please Mr Jellicon, sir, you don't mind if I take your paper-weight? It's my relative's bottom'? You've got to be joking!"

"But it's wrong that he should have Pete's pelvis," said Grandma. "It belongs on the seabed with the rest of his bones."

Pete nodded glumly.

"So you're suggesting I *steal* it?" said Theo.

"You can't steal something from a person when it

21

doesn't belong to them," said Grandma.

"You get it then!" cried Theo.

"We can't," said Grandma. "It's too much for us. We can do little things, now and again, but not anything like that."

"This is crazy!" said Theo. "I won't do it. Jellicon would never let me get away with it. I won't do it!"

"Alix will help you," said Grandma. "Where's Alix?"

A girl of about 13 slunk forward. She had bright-pink untidy hair and was wearing an old black leather jacket. She looked resentfully at Theo.

"Alix is not really dead," said Grandma.

"Not really dead? Oh, great!" said Theo. "That's all I need. A live dead person."

"She's not fully alive either. She got here by mistake. LIMBO looked after her. That's the Lost Infants and Motherless Babies Organization. She'll be a lot of help."

"No!" said Theo, eyeing Alix. He thought the only help she would give him was on the way to an accident.

"She can help in a way that the rest of us can't," said Grandma. "She's a bit stronger and—"

"Then get her to do it," said Theo. "Because I'm not."

Alix stuck out her tongue at Theo and wandered off. Pete and the other ghosts had all fallen silent.

"I'm disappointed in you, Theo," said Grandma.

"You always were, Grandma," said Theo.

"We're your relatives, Theo," said Grandma.

But Theo wasn't listening. He had turned and was making his way back towards the lift.

Rather to his surprise, Theo didn't hear from his grandma or any other ghosts for over a week. He began to wonder if they'd decided to leave him alone, though he scarcely dared hope that this was the case. It seemed far too unlikely, knowing his grandma. But the longer he was left alone, the more hopeful he became. Then, nine days after Grandma's visit, he had an appointment at the dentist's.

"Right, Theo, that's the X-rays done," said the dentist. "I'll just go and develop them. It won't take more than a few minutes."

Theo lay in the dentist's chair, staring at the ceiling. Somebody had thoughtfully stuck some pictures up there. He was studying one of a castle when he heard a strange moaning coming from somewhere near his feet.

"No! No! Stop!" went the moaning.

Theo sat up. There was a plump man kneeling by Theo's feet, wiggling what looked like a twiggy toilet brush. He was dressed in a greasy tunic, leather apron and cap, and on closer inspection Theo could see that his knees disappeared into the floor.

"Oh, here we go," muttered Theo. There wasn't any doubt. The man had a slight bluish glow around his body, only just visible in the bright light of the room. It was another ghost. "Who are you?"

"Wat," said the man.

"What?" said Theo.

"Yes, Wat," said the man. "Wat Kemp. I'm your first cousin, 14 times removed – at least, I think that's it."

"Ah," sighed Theo, wearily. "So Wat, what are you doing here?"

"I'm Trainee Second Assistant Apprentice Torturer. . ." said Wat, grinning. "Or I was, until I stood too close at an execution." He went back to tickling Theo's legs and moaning. "No, no. Stop!"

"Wat, what *are* you doing?" asked Theo.

"Tickling – I mean *torturing* you," said Wat. "Do you want me to stop?" He looked hopeful.

"I'm not ticklish, Wat. I can't feel a thing."

"Not even a tiny bit?"

Theo shook his head. Wat looked disappointed.

"Couldn't you just say the words?" said Wat.

Theo thought for a bit. Was his grandma losing her touch? This was ridiculous.

"OK, Wat. Have another go," he said.

Wat started tickling.

"No!" moaned Theo loudly. "Oh, no! Stop! Stop! I can't take any more."

The dentist looked round the door. "Theo, are you all right? I hope you don't think we'd deliberately hurt anyone here. . ."

"Oh no, Mrs Carlton. I'm fine, really. Thanks," said Theo.

"The X-rays are nearly ready." The dentist disappeared again.

"So, you'll do it?" said Wat.

"Do what, Wat?" said Theo.

"Get the bone. Pete's . . . you-know." Wat pointed to his backside.

"No, I won't!"

"Oh, pleeease," said Wat. "I promised them. I said I'd make you do it. I'd torture you till you said yes."

Theo looked at Wat and wondered about his

relatives. Were they all really so hopeless? He actually began to feel sorry for them.

"All right, Wat. I'll think about it," said Theo, before he realized what he was saying.

"You'll do it!" said Wat, grinning. "You'll do it!"

"I said I'll *think* about it. And I don't want any help from any ghosts or not-really-dead people."

The door opened and the dentist appeared holding the X-rays.

"I'm afraid you need a small filling, Theo," she said. "I'll do it now. It won't take a moment. Open wide, please."

Wat Kemp stood back, although the dentist couldn't see him.

"Do you mind if I stay and watch?" he whispered to Theo.

Theo tried to shake his head.

"Keep still, now, Theo," said the dentist. "I don't want to hurt you."

Have you ever said you will do something and then later regretted it? It's easily done. In a rash moment of generosity you say "yes I'll do that" and then realize, soon after, that you would rather not do it at all. But it's too late. You've said you will do the thing and you have to make the best of it. Or find an excuse and hope that people don't think too badly of you for getting out of it.

Theo found himself in this position. Of course, he'd only said he would think about trying to get back Pete's bottom, but he realized that that was pretty much the same as agreeing to have a go. To his credit, Theo didn't think of finding an excuse. But then he did want to try and get rid of his ghostly grandma for good. He hoped that getting back the bone would do the trick.

But how was he to do it? Theo considered the problem all the way back from the dentist's. The more he thought about it, the more Theo realized that perhaps the best way was to approach Mr Jellicon directly and ask him. Perhaps Jellicon would just laugh at him and tell him to go away. Theo was almost sure he would. But he thought he would give it a go, all the same.

Even this straightforward approach would not be easy. A busy and important man like Josiah Jellicon was hardly likely to give up some of his valuable time to see a boy like Theo. Not, that is, unless Theo had a very good reason. And so far, Theo couldn't think of a very good reason.

As Theo went in through the main doors of Vanilla Villas, he met the janitor, Mr Windrush, who had a room next to the entrance hall. Mr Windrush was a tall, thin man. He always walked with a slight stoop, as if expecting to bang his head on the ceiling, and he always carried a dustpan and brush. Mr Windrush was very fond of dust.

"Hello Mr Windrush," said Theo.

"Hello there," said Mr Windrush, who hardly ever called people by their names. He peered at Theo through his large, black-rimmed spectacles.

"How's the dust collection going?" asked Theo.

"Oh, it's coming on. I collected an excellent specimen from the town hall on Wednesday. From behind the clock. Very old and thick. And a most exceptional colour. That dust will have some tales to tell."

Mr Windrush firmly believed that dust held a record of all past time. The only thing that was needed was the right scientific system and the dust would reveal its secrets. History's most puzzling mysteries would be solved and Mr Windrush would be a famous man. He'd been working on a method for years but, so far, with only very limited success.

"How interesting," said Theo, who was not in the least interested.

"Yes, just look at this," said Mr Windrush, who reluctantly put down his dustpan so that he could open the door to his room and take a jar from a shelf. "Now look at that colour. That shows you the age. A preliminary test on the accumulation index gives a tentative date of 1863. And you see those bits?"

Theo peered at the grey mess inside the jar. "Yes. . ."

"Well, those are small pieces of leather," Mr Windrush said significantly.

Theo nodded as if he understood and cared.

"That Mr Jellicon's interested in my dust collection," went on Mr Windrush. "He telephoned after that newspaper article about me a couple of weeks ago. He said I should see what dust there was at the Jellicon factory."

"Really?" said Theo, who thought that Mr Jellicon must be having a joke at the janitor's expense. "That's wonderful, Mr Windrush."

Theo got into the lift. He went behind the curtain and sat on his bed while it travelled upwards. When the lift reached the third floor he got out and let himself into his family's flat. His mum was the only one there. His sisters were at one of their many music practice sessions and his dad was at work.

"Hello Mum," said Theo.

"Ваша черепаха находится в огне," said Theo's mum. She was lying on the sofa with headphones on, studying her Russian language tapes. Theo waved at her. "Та утка оченъ жирна," she said and blew him a kiss. Then she opened her mouth and pointed to her teeth. "How did you get on at the dentist?" she asked.

Theo leant over the sofa, opened his mouth very wide and showed her his new filling.

"Ah," said Theo's mum, nodding. She went back to her language tapes.

Theo went into the kitchen, still thinking about his conversation with Mr Windrush. As he was spreading a piece of bread with peanut butter, he had an idea. He got the phone book and found the number for Jellicon Comestibles. Then he picked up the phone, keyed in the number and waited.

"Jellicon Comestibles, good morning," said a voice.

Theo pinched his nose with his left hand in an effort to sound more like Mr Windrush. "I'd like to make an appointment to see Mr Jellicon."

"Hold on, I'll put you through," said the voice. There was a buzzing and then a new voice answered.

"Mr Jellicon's office, can I help you?" said the woman.

"I'd like to make an appointment to see Mr Jellicon," repeated Theo, still pinching his nose.

"Who is that, please?" said the woman.

"My name's Windrush," said Theo, pinching his nose hard.

There was a short pause and then the woman at Jellicon Comestibles spoke again.

"Oh yes, Mr Windrush, Mr Jellicon was hoping you'd ring."

"Oh?" said Theo, nearly forgetting to pinch his nose.

"Yes, only yesterday Mr Jellicon said he was so

much looking forward to seeing your collection of dust. Now then Mr Windrush, I've got the diary here. Would Wednesday at ten-thirty be all right?"

It was a moment before Theo could speak. "Yes, I think so."

"Good. We'll see you then," said the woman. "Don't forget your dustpan and brush."

The moment he had put the phone down Theo began to wonder if he hadn't been a little reckless in pretending to be Mr Windrush. He hadn't really expected Mr Jellicon to be so keen to see the dust collection. Theo didn't look a bit like the janitor. What if, on meeting him, Jellicon realized immediately that he was not the real Mr Windrush? Then there'd be some awkward explaining to do.

But Theo decided it was a risk worth taking. After all, he'd got what he had been hoping for: a meeting with Mr Jellicon. Theo tried to forget his misgivings. It was too good an opportunity to miss. As he sat down to eat his sandwich he started making plans.

Fortunately Theo had always enjoyed acting and had been in several plays at school. He knew that the key to a good performance was in the preparation. It was no good just speaking the lines. You had to *become* the character you were playing, behaving as they would, so that the audience forgot you were acting and believed you were that person. Theo spent the next few days preparing and perfecting his part.

"Are you all right, Theo?" asked his mum, when she found him sweeping out his sisters' bedrooms one evening.

"He's done something wrong," said Kate, one of the eldest twins. "It's just that you haven't found out yet."

"Yes, and why did he want all those jam jars?" said Louise, her twin sister. "Eight of them!"

"Seven," corrected Theo, who was brushing hard along the edge of a bookcase full of music books.

"I bet he's up to something," said Kate.

"I'm not!" protested Theo. "I'm just helping."

"Since when have you helped without being told to?" said Louise.

"Lots of times," said Theo. "When you were away singing silly songs."

"They're not silly!" cried the sisters.

"All right, all right, that's enough!" said Mrs Slugg. "I'm sure Theo knows they're not silly songs, girls.

And there's nothing wrong with Theo helping with the housework, if he wants to. Thank you, Theo," said Mrs Slugg and she went off to make herself a cup of coffee.

As you will no doubt have guessed, Theo had been collecting dust. His seven jam jars were arranged on a shelf above his bed. He'd labelled them with names such as *Railway Station* and *Mayor's Office*. Of course he'd not actually collected any dust from the railway station or mayor's office. It had all been collected from around the flat. But Theo thought the labels made the jars look more authentic. Except for in his own room, he'd had a hard time finding very much dust until he remembered the vacuum cleaner. He'd got four jars-full from emptying that.

Wednesday morning arrived, the day of the appointment with Mr Jellicon. When no one was looking, Theo borrowed his father's suit. It was several sizes too large but he thought it made him look a bit more grown up. An old pair of spectacles from a car boot sale completed the disguise. Looking in the mirror, Theo was very pleased with the effect. He put his jars of dust into his sports bag and pressed G for the ground floor.

Theo was just practising his Mr Windrush voice when the doors opened and there was nearly a nasty moment. Theo had forgotten all about the real Mr Windrush, who, as usual, was busy in his room next to the entrance hall. Theo darted behind a Swiss cheese plant and quickly took off the spectacles. He didn't want Mr Windrush asking any awkward questions. Fortunately the janitor was so busy sweeping, he didn't look up as Theo hurried out through the front doors, cursing himself for not being more careful.

At about ten-fifteen Theo arrived at the Jellicon Comestibles building. As he was early, he wandered up and down outside for a while, rehearsing his lines. He was a bit nervous about meeting Mr Jellicon. The man was so important in the town that nearly everyone was in awe of him, and now that Theo was about to meet him in person, he began to have second thoughts. He even thought about telephoning to say he was ill. But he didn't. Finally he plucked up courage and walked in through the shiny glass doors. There was a man behind a reception desk.

"I've come to see Mr Jellicon," said Theo.

"Got an appointment, have you?" said the man.

"Yes," said Theo. "For ten-thirty."

"Oooh," said the man, sucking through his teeth,

"I don't know about that. You see, there's a problem."

"What?" said Theo.

"The world's going to end at ten twenty-six." The man nodded towards a clock on the wall. It read ten twenty-five.

Theo didn't say anything. He and the man watched the clock as the seconds ticked by. Ten twenty-six arrived. Nothing happened.

"Huh," said the man, looking miserable. "Guess I was wrong. It happens. Second floor, reception desk on your right."

Theo went up the stairs. When he got to the second floor he went through the swing doors. A woman was sitting behind a desk typing away at a computer. She looked up at Theo but continued typing.

"I've come to see Mr Jellicon," said Theo.

"What name was it?" said the woman.

"Theo Sl-w-windrush," stammered Theo.

The woman stopped typing and looked at Theo closely for a moment. His heart missed a beat.

"Isn't that funny?" said the woman. "You were in the paper, weren't you? I could've sworn you were a tall man."

Theo swallowed hard and did his best to smile at

the woman. To his great relief, she picked up the phone and said, "Mr Jellicon, Mr Windrush is here to see you." Then she put down the phone and turned to Theo. "He won't be a moment, Mr Windrush."

Theo sat down to wait. There was a large screen on the wall showing advertisements for Jellicon Comestibles. Theo watched a troupe of animated jam jars dance about in a golden countryside. To his disgust, the jam jars started to sing:

"We're Jellicon's jams, here for your convenience,
Each one's made with the finest ingredients!
We're the best!
We're the best!
When put to the test
Jellicon's jams are ALWAYS the BEST!"

The ads didn't say anything about the artificial raspberry pips that Theo's dad made. And they didn't mention seaweed.

Theo had to wait for about five minutes and then the woman showed him into Mr Jellicon's office.

The office was vast. There was a thick white carpet on the floor. Theo thought it was like walking on the back of an enormous shaggy dog. The few bits of furniture were modern pieces made of glass and stainless steel. At first Theo didn't see Mr Jellicon. Then he appeared from behind a gigantic fish tank.

"Ah, Mr Windrush, how good of you to come," boomed Jellicon, coming forward to shake Theo's hand. He shook it so violently that Theo began to wonder if his arm would come off. "I find this dust stuff fascinating, fascinating. You're welcome to collect all the dust you want here – and for free . . . probably. . . You did bring some with you? Good! Do sit down."

Theo sat down. The huge chair was very soft and he sank so far into it that he nearly disappeared. He struggled upright and then opened his sports bag. He began to take out his jam jars.

"This sample was collected from the railway station," explained Theo. He did his best to make his voice sound whiny, like the janitor's, but of course this time he had to do it without pinching his nose. "You see that grey colour? Well that shows you the age. My initial estimate is 1750."

"Really?" said Jellicon, taking the jar in his large hands and peering at it closely. "Fascinating. And maybe, with the right flavourings . . . who knows. . ."

"And this one is from the mayor's office," Theo went on.

Then he realized Jellicon was staring at him.

"Funny, I could have sworn you were a tall man. . ." rumbled Jellicon. "But wait. . . You're not Windrush! Windrush *is* a tall man. I remember his photo in the paper." Jellicon leapt up, all the niceness gone. "*Who are you? What are you doing here?*"

Theo shrank back into the chair, wishing he could disappear. He decided it was probably time to tell the truth. It was a moment before he could find his voice. "My name's Theo Slugg."

"Slugg? Don't I know that name?" thundered Jellicon. But he shook his head; he couldn't think why the name was familiar. "Well? And this had better be good."

"I've come about . . . a paperweight," whispered Theo. He looked around the room but couldn't see Pete's bottom anywhere.

Mr Jellicon looked fierce. "And what paperweight would that be?"

"It's a bone," said Theo, his voice squeaky with anxiety. He felt like a mouse facing a tiger. "It belongs to Pete Pilkington. It's his bottom."

Mr Jellicon sat down behind his desk and stared

41

at Theo. He said nothing for a minute-and-a-half.

"Let me see that I've got this right. You're telling me that I've got a paperweight and this paperweight is actually the bone of a man's bottom, a man called Pete Pingleton?"

"Pilkington," corrected Theo.

"Ah," said Jellicon. "And this man Pilkington wants the bone back?"

Theo nodded.

Jellicon looked hard at Theo. "This Pete Pilkington. Where is he exactly?"

"He's . . . dead," mumbled Theo, looking down at the shaggy white carpet.

"He's dead," repeated Jellicon. "So why would he want it back then?"

"Because he can't dance properly without it," explained Theo. "You see, he's Fast Feet Pete, the famous tap-dancer and he can't dance properly without his bottom. His legs keep wandering off."

"But you said he was dead," said Jellicon. "Are you telling me that although he's dead, he can still dance?"

"Yes – no – but –" gibbered Theo.

"I see," said Jellicon. "So we should look out because the dead will soon be dancing in the

42

streets. . .? Now look here, Mr Wind – Slugg – whatever your name is, I'm a very busy man. I have not got time to talk nonsense with someone who believes in dead people dancing."

"Yes," squeaked Theo.

"And you've got some cheek coming in here pretending to be someone else. Do you think I'm a fool?"

"No," gasped Theo.

"I'm an important man and you've wasted my time," went on Jellicon. "But I'm also a very reasonable man, Mr Slush. . . And, on this occasion, I'll be *very very* reasonable. . . You've got courage. I admire that. . . On consideration, you can have the paperweight."

It took a moment for Jellicon's words to sink in. Theo could hardly believe his luck. He stood up unsteadily. "Wow!"

"Yes, it's in the fish tank," said Jellicon, who had begun sorting some papers on his desk. "You can take it whenever you want."

Theo looked at the fish tank. There, lying in the sand at the bottom, was the bone of a man's bottom. Half a dozen plump fish were swimming about nearby. Was the man joking? He'd said he could take it. Theo shrugged. He took off his dad's jacket and

43

rolled up his shirt sleeves. Then he walked over to the fish tank.

"Ah, I wouldn't do that if I were you," said Jellicon, standing up. "Watch this."

Jellicon took an apple from a bowl of fruit on his desk and dropped it into the fish tank. Instantly the water was churned as the fish jostled each other to get a bite. In less than thirty seconds the apple was reduced to a small bit of stalk floating on the water surface.

"Yellow Diamond Piranhas," said Jellicon, proudly. "Voracious eaters from the Amazon. If that's what they can do to an apple, imagine what they'd do to your arm." He grinned ferociously at Theo and then went over to his desk. He pressed a button on the telephone. "Miss Moulder, show Mr Windrugg out, if you would, please."

"Arghh!" cried Theo, kicking an empty drinks can. There was a loud "clang" as it bounced off a gravestone.

Theo was taking the short cut home through the cemetery. He was furious. He couldn't believe how Jellicon had tricked him.

"Now, that's no way to behave," said a voice beside him. It was Theo's grandma.

"Oh, that's all I need," muttered Theo.

"No respect for the dead," grumbled Grandma. "It will land you in trouble."

"Grandma, I've had enough!" moaned Theo.

"So you didn't get it?"

"No, I didn't!" Theo kicked the can again.

"What a surprise!" said Grandma. "Hopeless little

worm. You thought you were so clever. 'I'll do it my way' you said. Ha, ha. And where did that get you?"

"You said it was a paperweight," protested Theo. "Well it's not. It's in a fish tank with a lot of man-eating piranhas."

"If you'd done it my way, it would have worked," said Grandma.

"Oh really? How?" said Theo. "That half-dead girl good at fishing?"

"She might be. She's clever. You should try again with her help and find out. As I always say, if at first you don't succeed. . ."

"No!"

"Rude boy!" exclaimed Grandma.

Theo started to walk on, leaving his grandma sitting on a gravestone.

An old man who had been putting flowers on a grave looked at him strangely. Theo realized he must have heard him talking to what seemed like thin air. Theo gave him a smile but the old man hurried off in the opposite direction.

"See how you upset people?" shouted Grandma. "You should have more consideration for your elders. Mark my words, you'll be sorry!"

Theo took no notice and kept walking along the path.

He glimpsed other ghosts among the gravestones. Wat Kemp, in his greasy cap and apron, was among them. He waved at Theo and hurried over.

"Did you get it?" asked Wat, looking hopeful.

Theo shook his head and kept on walking.

"But you'll have another go, won't you?" said Wat, shambling alongside.

"I don't think so, Wat," said Theo.

"Go on, you can do it. I know you can."

"No I can't, Wat. It's too difficult."

Wat looked very disappointed. He slumped down on the steps of an ornate monument which had a stone angel on the top. The other ghosts gathered round, all looking very sad and thin in the morning sunlight. It reminded Theo of an old family photograph he'd once seen in a leather-bound album. It had been brown and faded so you couldn't see the faces clearly.

Then Theo noticed Pete Pilkington, standing slightly apart from the rest, beside a clipped yew tree. He had his hands firmly in his pockets and looked the saddest of all. Theo felt he should say something and went over.

"I'm sorry, Pete. I did try. Really, I did."

Pete looked at Theo with his sad bulgy eyes, his lower lip quivering.

"That's all right, Theo, my friend. I know you did your best. Please don't you trouble yourself over it any more. You go along home now."

Theo's mood sank even further. He turned away and hurried on along the path.

Just as he was leaving the cemetery he saw the not-really-dead girl, Alix, her untidy pink hair blowing in the breeze. She was swinging a bit of rusty chain. She grinned at Theo, then picked her nose, flicking her finger in his direction. Theo took no notice but walked briskly out through the gates.

When he got home, Theo went and lay on his bed. He needed to think. His plan was to abandon the whole tiresome enterprise. Grandma wouldn't like it and she'd make life unpleasant for him but Theo thought she'd go away eventually. She'd have to. He could be stubborn when he felt like it. He'd just refuse to do what she wanted. She'd have to admit defeat.

But as Theo turned it over in his mind, the more he thought that he couldn't just leave it like that, with Pete bottomless. He began to think that perhaps he'd have another go. There was something about Wat's disappointment and Pete's sad look that made him want to try again. A small part of him even wanted to please his grandma, although he didn't know why. Perhaps the fact that she was part of his family really mattered, after all. And on top of all that, Jellicon's mean trick had made him angry. Jellicon had said he could take the bone whenever he wanted – so he would!

The problem was: how? It wasn't going to be easy. He couldn't go and see Jellicon and ask him again. Somehow he'd have to get into Jellicon's office and get the bone from the fish tank. Theo thought hard.

Have you ever noticed how sometimes, when you've got a particularly thorny problem to solve, thinking about other things helps? You stop thinking about whatever it is, do something else and after a little while, without you thinking about it at all, the solution to the problem pops out of the blue, all by itself.

Theo sat gazing at his bed, his books and the pictures in his part of the lift and he suddenly became aware of how tidy everything looked after his dust-collecting efforts. Although Mr Windrush cleaned the part of the lift where people stood, he never touched

Theo's part. It had never looked so clean. That didn't suit him at all. He liked his room to have a lived-in look, not be too tidy. So he started messing things up a bit, to make it all more comfortable. While pulling a few books off his bookshelf, he found that he'd left the dustpan and brush at the bottom of his bed. And it was then that the idea came to him.

Boldness is the key to success. With enough daring the most unlikely plans can be carried off. You just need courage and a cool head. Then nothing is impossible.

Luck helps, of course.

Now Theo had a plan. He'd thought hard about it and, with a little bit of luck, he might just be able to carry it off. He'd asked his dad a few questions about the routine at Jellicon Comestibles, while being careful not to make him suspicious, and by Thursday evening he was all ready.

At half-past five the next morning, Theo was outside the Jellicon building. He went straight up to the front door and rapped on the glass. After a moment, the security guard came over. Theo was relieved to see that it was a different man from his last visit.

"Yes?" said the man without opening the door. Theo could barely hear him.

"*Hello,*" shouted Theo, "*I'm supposed to be starting as a cleaner this morning.*"

"What?" bawled the man, who obviously hadn't heard a word.

"I'm supposed to be starting as a cleaner," shouted Theo again, this time a little less loudly.

The security man, who naturally still couldn't hear, shook his head wearily and opened the door. Theo explained why he was there.

"Blimey, you're early," said the man. "The others don't turn up much before six. And Mr Clinker won't be here until ten past. He's always late. He's the one that'll tell you what to do."

"Could I come in?" asked Theo. "I need to use the – you know. . ."

"Hmm, I don't know about that. I'm not supposed to let anybody in outside regulation hours – not unless they've got a special pass."

"Pleeease," begged Theo.

"Where's your card?"

"They haven't given me one yet, as it's my first day." Theo hopped from one leg to the other.

"Oh, all right," said the man, pulling back the door.

"The gents is down the corridor, on the right."

Theo hurried inside and locked himself in a cubicle. He sat down and waited for a bit to make his excuse seem realistic, then he pressed the flush, washed and dried his hands and went back out to the entrance hall. The security man was sitting behind the desk.

"Thanks," said Theo, sitting down on a chair. He hoped the security man wouldn't ask him to wait outside.

"You're welcome," said the man.

"Do you have to look after this place on your own?" asked Theo, a few minutes later.

"Eh? Yes, this shift. There are two on nights, usually," answered the man, who was looking at the security monitors.

"It's a lot for one person to look after, isn't it?" said Theo.

"Oh yes!" agreed the man, who liked complaining. "There should be more of us really. The place is big enough. But the boss won't allow it. Waste of resources, he says."

"But what hard work for you!" said Theo.

"It is," said the man with a wry grin.

Theo picked up a magazine from a low table. It was called *Jam Today*. He was just looking at some pictures of the latest jam-making machinery when the security man leapt out of his chair.

"*What the* –?" yelled the man, staring at a screen. "Oh bother! There's something going on in the factory. I expect it's only those dodgy lights again but I'm sorry, I'll have to shut you outside while I go and investigate."

Theo went back outside, the security man shut the door behind him and then hurried off down the corridor. Theo stood peering in through the glass door, wondering what to do. It was going to be more difficult getting into Jellicon's office than he'd thought. He'd been stupid to think he'd just have to say he was a cleaner and would be let straight in. He leant against the glass, trying to think up a new plan, and nearly fell over as the door swung inwards.

Thankful that the security man had not locked it properly, Theo closed the door behind him and hurried over to the security monitors. He could see the man walking into the factory at the back of the building. Now was his chance, if he was quick. . .

Theo dashed up the stairs to the second floor and a minute later he was outside the door to Jellicon's office. He went inside, closing the door quietly behind him, and crossed to the fish tank. The fish were gathered at one end. Theo hoped that they were sleeping, although with fish it is difficult to tell. From his bag he took out a ball of string and a large hook that he'd made from a wire coathanger. He pulled across a chair to stand on so that he could reach over the tank and started lowering the hook into the water.

It was nervous work. Theo worried that the fish would get interested and leap out of the water, taking bites out of him. His hands trembled and sweat dripped off him into the water.

At last the hook hit the bottom and Theo dragged it across, trying to catch hold of the bone. It was fiddly work but at the third attempt he managed it. He pulled the string and, slowly, up came the bone. Theo tried not to rush it. The fish seemed to have woken up and were now mooning about. Theo couldn't help noticing how sharp their teeth were. He wondered anxiously if they were hungry.

Just as Theo was about to lift out the bone, a dark shape loomed on the other side of the tank. Theo was so surprised he lurched backwards, letting go of the string, and crashing off the chair.

Then the alarm bells started to ring.

"Ow," said Theo, rubbing his head. He'd fallen hard on to the floor. He looked up to see Wat Kemp leaning over him.

"Wat! It's you! You idiot, you made me drop the bone! And I nearly had the thing." Pete's pelvis was back at the bottom of the fish tank. Theo's hook and string were alongside it in the sand.

"I was only trying to help," wailed Wat.

"Like how? Argh! Useless family!"

Theo scrambled to his feet crossly, his head thumping. With the alarm bells ringing somebody would be there at any moment. "I'd better get out of here."

"I could see if anybody's coming," said Wat, desperate to make amends.

"But then you'll get caught," said Theo, irritably.

And then he remembered that as Wat was a ghost the security man wouldn't see him. "Yes, Wat, good idea. Go and have a quick look. Thanks."

Wat hurried through the wall of the office. He was back in a moment.

"All clear."

Cautiously Theo opened the door. He couldn't see anybody by the desk and the passage was empty. If only the alarm bells would stop their racket, then he'd be able to hear if anybody was approaching. He thought the best plan would be to go back the way he had come, down the stairs. The lift would be too risky. It would be a disaster to get caught that way. He set off.

Just as Theo reached the top of the stairs he saw a hand move on the rail below. Somebody was coming up. Theo spun round and dodged into the nearest room. It was a small kitchen.

"It's all right. They didn't see you," said Wat, joining him. He stood with his body going through the work surface. The kettle's spout stuck out of the middle of his apron.

"Wat, why did you have to do that?" asked Theo. He could talk freely. With the bells still ringing throughout the building, nobody would hear.

"What?" said Wat.

"Why did you suddenly appear behind the fish tank, just when I almost had Pete's bone? You totally spooked me. You ruined everything!"

"I was only trying to help." Wat looked very unhappy. "Your grandma, she said—"

"Grandma!" cried Theo. "So she suggested you help? I might have known."

Wat looked miserable. "She said to keep an eye on you. I only meant. . ."

"Yes, Wat. It's all right, I know." Theo was furious. What was his grandma up to? Did she want him to fail? Theo couldn't work it out. But he hadn't time to worry about it now. He had to get out of the building.

"Have another look, Wat. See if they've gone."

Wat disappeared through the wall. He seemed to be gone for ages and Theo began to wonder if he was ever coming back. Then Wat stuck his head through the door.

"All clear," he said. "The man's gone the other way."

"Good. Then here I go."

Theo darted out of the kitchen and down the stairs. When he got to the bottom he paused to see if there was anyone in the reception area but it was empty. As long as the main door was still unlocked, he could escape. Theo ran to the door and pulled on the handle. He was in luck. The door swung inwards. He was free. Theo dashed outside, down the steps and then ran as fast as he could around the corner. Slap bang into a policeman.

"Oof!" gasped the policeman. He caught hold of Theo, who was trying to wriggle away. "And where do you think you're going in such a hurry? . . . Those jingling bells I can hear wouldn't be anything to do with you, would they?"

"Me? Oh, no officer!" gulped Theo. "I'm just going shopping."

"Hmm, and I'm Father Christmas," said the policeman. "You're coming with me, lad."

As the policeman was the size of a small bus and had a very firm grip on Theo's arm, Theo decided that it was best to do as he was told. He was marched back to the Jellicon Comestibles building. As they went in through the door, the security man switched off the alarm.

"Ah, hello officer," said the security man. "Thank

goodness! I see you've caught the criminal. He nipped into Mr J's office when my back was turned. Trying to steal some of his valuable fish, he was."

"Really?" said the policeman. He didn't relax his grip on Theo.

"Yes, Yellow Diamond Piranhas they are. Very valuable."

"I wasn't!" protested Theo.

"He pretended to be a cleaner!"

"Did he?" said the policeman. "But you weren't fooled?"

"Not for a minute," answered the security man, looking uncomfortable.

"Hmm," said the policeman, turning his attention to Theo. He seemed satisfied that Theo was not about to run for it and sat him down in a chair. Then he took a notebook and pencil from a pocket in his uniform. "Now then, young man," he said, "you're in deep custard. What made you think you could walk in and take some of Mr Jellicon's fish?"

"I didn't," said Theo. "I don't want any of his horrid fish."

"Yes, he did!" chirped the security man, sure of himself again. "There's his fish-hook and string in the tank! I saw them."

"Hmm?" said the policeman to Theo.

"That wasn't for the fish," said Theo. "That was for the bone. The bone doesn't belong to Mr Jellicon. He found it in the sea. But it belongs to someone else."

"You're not going to believe that, are you?" said the guard. "He's having you on."

"What bone is this?" asked the policeman.

"It's Pete Pilkington's," said Theo. "He was a tap-dancer."

"Hmm," said the policeman, who was writing it all down in his notebook.

"He's one of my relatives," said Theo. "I said I'd get the bone back for him."

"Ah," said the policeman, who in his long career in the force had come across many strange things. He was now hardly ever surprised by anything. "And your name is?"

"Theo Slugg," said Theo.

The policeman stopped writing. His expression changed from uniform grey to sunny cheerfulness. "You're not related to those singers are you? What are they called. . .? The Singing Sluggs, isn't it?"

"Yes, they're my sisters," mumbled Theo, with an uncomfortable sense of foreboding.

62

"Never heard of them," said the security man, flatly.

"What? Really?" said the policeman, astonished. "My wife, she loves their singing. She could listen to them for hours. What's that song? The one they always sing. . ."

"Never liked music," said the security man, tetchily.

Theo shook his head vigorously.

"No, you must know it," said the policeman. "Cherry trees or something . . . how does it go now?" The policeman began to hum and Theo felt queasy. "There, that's how it goes. Of course you know it. Sing it for us!"

"I can't sing," croaked Theo. He'd gone green.

"Course you can," said the policeman, who wasn't going to be put off.

With a sick feeling of despair, Theo realized that there was no getting out of it. He briefly considered making a dash for the door but decided that would only make matters worse. He stood up shakily, took a couple of deep breaths and began to sing:

> *"The cherry blossom on the trees,*
> *Is swinging gaily in the breeze,*
> *And little birdies sweetly sing*
> *Of happy days and bits of string."*

The policeman, his eyes closed, waved his hand in the air and swayed slightly in time to the tune. The security man looked on in disgust.

"Don't stop," whispered the policeman, dreamily.

Theo gulped down another deep breath.

> *"It is the springtime of the year,*
> *The cooey doves are full of cheer.*
> *The busy bees their honey make,*
> *Their little wings must surely ache!"*

Theo was appalled to see that the cleaners had started to arrive. They formed a semi-circle around him and stood listening. Wat had reappeared and was standing with them, a smile on his face. He seemed to be enjoying Theo's discomfort.

Theo's stomach churned. Desperately he went on.

> *"In grassy meadows flowers sway,*
> *Where sheep and cattle pass the day.*
> *The bunnies frolic in the sun,*
> *And dodge the farmer with his gun.*

Meanwhile the fox, back at the farm,
Counts the chickens, free from harm.
All things are jolly in the spring,
And that's the end now, ding-a-ling!"

Everybody except the security man clapped. Theo went deep pink.

"Now get along home, lad," said the policeman, who was all smiles. He pointed Theo in the direction of the door and gave him a shove. "And stay out of mischief."

"Hey! But –" spluttered the security man.

Theo heard the policeman begin to say something about "not a bad lad" but that was all. He wasn't going to wait around in case the policeman changed his mind and hauled him off to the police station. He stumbled towards the door in a bit of a daze, but the moment he was outside he dashed around the corner, and he didn't stop running until he'd reached Luigi's Café, where he slumped into a chair. He needed some breakfast.

Luigi's was a favourite haunt of Theo's. It was run by a man called Nigel, who made the best ice cream for a hundred miles around. Rather like a small cave, the café was decorated with a lot of empty wine bottles and bits of old fishing net. A big mirror ran the length of one wall. On the opposite wall there was a mural painting of the seaside with a few slightly wonky seagulls and some rubbery-looking rocks.

"You are very early today, Mr Theo," said Nigel, who liked to affect an Italian accent, although all his relatives for the last five hundred years had been born in Essex.

"Yes," said Theo. "I slept badly."

"I think you not look well, my friend. A Luigi's special pancake will make you feel better, yes?" said Nigel, wiping down Theo's table with a grey cloth.

"Yes, please, Nigel," said Theo. A special pancake, which came with ice cream, would be just the thing to help him recover.

"I get it for you," said Nigel, and he went off to the kitchen.

While he waited, Theo sat leaning against the big mirror. He stared absent-mindedly around the café. He was the only customer.

"Well, you made a right muck of that, didn't you?" said a voice over his shoulder.

Theo swung round to look in the mirror. Of course, it was Grandma. In the reflection, she was sitting in one of the chairs opposite him but when Theo looked to see if she really was opposite, the seat was empty. Grandma was only in the mirror.

"Oh yes, clever clogs, you really made a pig's whisker of it this time, didn't you?" she said.

"How did you find out so fast?" asked Theo. "Oh, don't tell me – Wat told you."

Grandma nodded. There was a satisfied look on her face. "He has his uses."

"So you sent him to help me?"

Grandma smiled.

"Well, thank you very much," said Theo. "If he

67

hadn't shown up just at that moment, I probably would have got it."

Grandma's smile broadened. Theo stared at her.

"You *did* want me to fail, didn't you?" he cried, angrily. "Just so that you'd be proved right."

"Mr Theo, my friend, are you all right?" It was Nigel. Theo hadn't noticed him come out from the kitchen, he'd been so angry with Grandma.

"Oh . . . yes," said Theo, quickly. "Thank you."

"You know what they say, my friend. . ." said Nigel, putting Theo's pancake and a glass of cola on the table.

"What?" asked Theo.

"People that talk to themselves," said Nigel, wiggling his hand at the side of his head. "Screwy, no?" Naturally Nigel couldn't see Grandma.

"Er . . . yes," muttered Theo, trying to think. "Don't worry, Nigel. I've . . . this thing . . . to learn for school."

"Ah," said Nigel, nodding. He looked relieved. "So that's it. The play acting. It is hard work, is it not, the learning of the lines?"

"Oh yes!" exclaimed Theo. "Very hard work."

"And for actors, a little luck is good, is it not?" went on Nigel, warming to his theme. "I wish you luck, my friend. I wish you the breaking of a leg!"

"Thanks, Nigel," said Theo, trying to sound cheerful. He knew that "break a leg" was an actor's expression for good luck but he'd always thought it odd. He heard Grandma snigger behind him.

"Enjoy your pancake, Mr Theo," said Nigel, smiling. He went back into the kitchen.

Grandma started giggling. "Fancy you having to sing for the copper! *That* must have been a performance!" she chortled.

"Stop it!" hissed Theo. "You're horrid. And don't think I'm going to do things your way, because I'm not. I don't care if you send all the toads in Deadland, I'm not doing any more. It's finished. Over. So you can go away."

"That's no way to talk to your grandma."

"You always wanted to control me," said Theo, trying to keep his voice down and an eye on the café. It was still empty but he didn't want to risk upsetting any of Nigel's customers. "Well, I've had enough. I want to lead my own life, not do what you want the whole time. I tried to get back Pete's bottom for you. I tried twice, and would've succeeded if you hadn't spoilt things. Give me one good reason why I should try again."

"Don't you love your family?" said Grandma.

69

"Argh!" groaned Theo. "Why should I care about a lot of dead relatives? You never did much for me when you were alive. Why should I care about you now? Or any of those other ugly losers?" Theo had started eating his pancake but he hardly noticed the taste, he was so angry. Even the ice cream made no impression.

"Typical," said Grandma. "You always were a self-ish boy."

"I'm not! You just won't let me —" spluttered Theo. A piece of pancake shot out of his mouth, straight towards Grandma. It hit the mirror and stuck there.

"Disgusting," grumbled Grandma. "Where are your table manners? Anyway, you'll come round to the idea." She looked smug.

Theo felt uneasy. Grandma obviously had another plan up her sleeve. He regarded her with suspicion. Then he noticed a movement in the mirror. It was the not-really-dead girl, Alix. Theo glanced round at the real café but the girl was only in the reflection like his grandma.

Grandma turned around. "Ah, there she is. Alix, come here."

Alix had started prancing around on one of the tables at the back of the café, exploring the wine bottles and netting. She was wearing heavy black boots and making quite a mess of the tablecloth. In her hair was what looked like a dead crow. She didn't take any notice of Grandma.

"Alix, come here," repeated Grandma.

Alix went on examining the empty wine bottles.

"Alix, will you come here!" growled Grandma. She got up and hobbled over to Alix, waving her stick. Finally Alix slunk over to the table and sat down sulkily.

"Now then," said Grandma, once she was back in her chair, "this is the plan. First Alix will look at the building to find the best way in, check out the security, that sort of thing. Then she will—"

"Won't," muttered Alix.

"What?" said Grandma.

"I won't," said Alix, staring at the table. "I won't do it."

Theo sat up.

"Don't talk nonsense. Of course you will," said Grandma. "Then you will—"

"No, I won't," said Alix, getting up. "I'm not helping. I've had enough of your plans."

"Don't be silly," said Grandma. "Now, sit down."

"No," said Alix, climbing on to the table. She

tramped across the table top towards Theo. To his surprise, she didn't stop at the mirror but pushed her way through to his side. There was a strange sucking noise as she passed through. His mouth open, Theo watched her muddy boots cross the table. As she put her foot down near him, she knocked over his drink. The liquid went everywhere and Theo had to leap out of the way. Alix gave him a smirk, jumped off the table and ran out of the café.

Nigel came over with a cloth. He'd seen the drink go over, but as he couldn't see Alix, he thought Theo had spilt it by accident.

"The drink knocked over itself, yes?" he said kindly, mopping up the liquid.

"Er . . . yes," said Theo, who was still trying to take in what had just happened.

"Never mind," said Nigel. "I get you another."

For a moment Grandma said nothing. Then she got up, mumbling to herself. "Hmm. So she won't help, will she? Well, we'll see about that." She started to walk away from Theo, towards the "other" café door in the mirror, but then she stopped and looked back at him. "And you can wipe that smile off your face!"

Theo watched his Grandma's ghost disappear. He

couldn't help himself, he was grinning broadly. He felt better than he had done for days.

"You enjoy the pancake, yes?" said Nigel. "It make you feel better?"

"Yes, Nigel," said Theo. "I think I'll have another."

Theo was delighted that Alix's behaviour at the café that morning had obviously taken Grandma completely by surprise. But he realized that she wasn't likely to be thwarted for long. She just wasn't the sort to give up that easily.

By the afternoon, he'd begun to get a little anxious as to what she would try next. He was in no doubt that his grandma would be planning something nasty and that he'd be on the receiving end.

At half-past six that evening, Theo was having supper with his family. He really liked mealtimes. It wasn't just the food; it was also that his sisters couldn't sing with their mouths full.

"Theo, don't eat so fast," said Mrs Slugg.

"Sobby Mum," slurped Theo.

"And don't speak with your mouth full," said Mr Slugg.

Theo's dad had done the cooking. It was spaghetti Bolognese, one of Theo's favourites. Both Theo's parents were good cooks but since starting her Russian course, Theo's mum had cooked rather a lot of meals with beetroot in them. Theo was enjoying not having to eat beetroot for the first time in six nights.

"Dad," asked Theo between mouthfuls, "is it always raspberry pips that you make at work?"

"Mostly," answered Mr Slugg. "Sometimes it's strawberry pips and very occasionally plum stones but raspberry jam is the most popular. Research has shown that the jam sells better if there are more pips in it than occur naturally."

"So there are *real* raspberries in the jam?"

Mr Slugg looked shocked. "Oh yes."

"But Theo, you know it says 'finest ingredients' on the labels," said Mrs Slugg. "That means real raspberries."

"So you've *seen* the raspberries have you, Dad?" persisted Theo, who wasn't so sure.

"Well, no. . ." said Mr Slugg. "The fruit is processed in a different part of the factory."

75

"Waagghh!" wailed Emily, the youngest of all the Slugg sisters. "Waaagggghhh!"

Everybody looked round. Emily was pointing at her plate. Hannah, who was sitting next to her, started screaming too.

"What is it, darlings?" cried Mrs Slugg, rushing over to her daughters.

There was a spider in Emily's spaghetti. It was only a plastic spider but it made her scream all the same. Mrs Slugg put a comforting arm around both her and Hannah.

"It's Theo's spider," said Kate. "He must have put it there."

"Theo!" cried Mrs Slugg. "Why on earth did you do such a thing?"

"I didn't!" protested Theo. It did *look* like his spider but he thought he'd lost it, ages ago. He'd no idea how it had turned up in Emily's spaghetti.

"Of course you did it," said Kate. "You knew it would make Emily cry. You know how she hates spiders."

"Really, I didn't do it," said Theo.

"Well, if you didn't, who did?" said Kate. As one of the eldest of Theo's sisters she always defended the others against their brother.

"*Grandma!*" Theo muttered under his breath.

"That's silly," said Kate, who'd heard. "How could Grandma do it?"

"That's an awful thing to say," said Mrs Slugg. "I'm glad Grandma's not here to hear you say that."

"I didn't mean –" began Theo but he realized it was too late.

"He always was a naughty boy," muttered Grandma as if everyone could hear her. "Always playing tricks of this sort." She'd walked into the room and was standing with her body going through the television set. A vase of flowers stuck out of her dress. Only Theo knew she was there. Only he could see her.

"That's enough, Theo," said Mr Slugg. "Now apologize to Emily."

"But I didn't do it!"

"A bad boy like him? Of course he did it!" said Grandma. She grinned meanly at Theo. "Always playing tricks on his sisters."

"You shouldn't play tricks on your sisters," said Mrs Slugg.

Theo couldn't believe it. It was almost as if his mother had heard Grandma. He hardly *ever* played tricks on his sisters. She knew he didn't.

"But I promise, it wasn't me!" he groaned.

77

Grandma looked triumphant. Theo knew it had been her doing, though how she'd managed to get the spider into the food he didn't know. She looked so pleased, gloating at his misfortune, it made him furious. She was only doing it out of spite. Just because he wouldn't do what she wanted, she was making life unpleasant for him. Well then, he'd show her! He must try to remain cool. He got up and went over to Emily.

"Sorry Emily," he said, using his best apologetic voice. "I didn't mean to scare you. The spider must have fallen out of my pocket by mistake, when I was carrying the plates in. . ."

"That's better," said Mrs Slugg.

"What do you mean?" cried Grandma, in dismay. "You're not going to let the weaselly wombat get away with it, are you? He's not really sorry you know! You can see he's not!"

"All right Theo, we'll forget all about it," said Mr Slugg.

"Over my dead body!" cried Grandma. She was furious. "Send him to bed early! Lock him in a cupboard! That's what the hideous little newt deserves!"

"Theo didn't really mean it, did he, Dad?" asked Lizzie.

"That's right."

"Huh!" exclaimed Grandma, crossly. "Hopeless load of horsetails!" And she stomped off, whacking her stick on the floor as she went.

Theo woke up on Sunday morning feeling cheerful. He'd slept well, with no visits from his grandma or any of the other ghosts. And although he thought Grandma would still be planning some nastiness – she'd regard his and Alix's disobedience as only a temporary setback – for the time being, she was leaving him alone.

At about ten-thirty the lift started travelling downwards. Someone on a lower floor had pressed the button. When the lift stopped on the ground floor, Theo peeped round his curtain to see who it was. It was Mr Windrush.

"Hello there," said Mr Windrush, as he got in. As well as his dustpan and brush, he was carrying a bucket of cloths ready to clean the stairwell windows, a job he often did on a Sunday.

"Hello, Mr Windrush," said Theo, jumping up. As he did so, his foot kicked something under his bed. It hit the wall of the lift and then rolled out in front of Mr Windrush.

It was a jam jar. Mr Windrush picked it up.

"I didn't know you were collecting dust!" exclaimed Mr Windrush, looking at the jar. There was a label stuck to the outside. It said *Railway Station*.

"Er . . . no," stammered Theo, going pink. "I was going to . . . but I've been so busy. . ."

"How interesting," murmured Mr Windrush, who was studying the dust very closely. "This dust, you know . . . it has the most exceptional notes . . . just as if. . . But surely not?"

"What?" said Theo, wondering what he was talking about.

"Notes!" said Mr Windrush. "Definitely. There's no doubt."

"What sort of notes?" asked Theo.

"Why, *musical* notes, of course!" said Mr Windrush. "It's surprising but someone has definitely been singing at the railway station."

The lift reached the third floor. Mr Windrush handed the jam jar to Theo. "I'd like to see more of your collection, when you're not so busy," he said, as he picked up his things.

"Oh," gulped Theo. "All right, Mr Windrush."

Later that day, when Theo was going to bed, he discovered a piece of paper on his pillow. It was very flimsy. He had a lot of difficulty picking it up. He couldn't grip it, his fingers kept passing straight through the paper. It was a ghost letter.

It read:

Dear Theo,

We the undersinged, being yor beluved family, imploor you to reconsidder yor deesidjun. Pete needs his bottom sumthing awful. He is misery without it and cannot danse either. Pleas help. It will be wurth yor wile.

If yu will, be at the Plarzer at half past midnight tomorrer. Alicks will be thur.

Thank yu.

Yor luving family

PS Yor grandma dusn't know weeve ritten.

There were a lot of names at the bottom, none of which Theo recognized, and quite a few crosses.

Theo knew the crosses were the marks of people who couldn't write their names.

At first Theo didn't know what to think. His grandma's name wasn't on the letter. She didn't seem to have had anything to do with it. And anyway, letters weren't really her style. He didn't know any of the names on the list but there were several Sluggs and he was certain the others were all his relations, from goodness knows how long ago. He had to admit that he was impressed that they'd organized them-selves to write. Especially as Grandma didn't seem to be behind it. Perhaps his family weren't quite as use-less as he'd thought.

He lay awake for almost an hour thinking about what to do. The Plaza was the cinema in town. He could easily get there after midnight. Perhaps he would do it, not for Grandma but for his family.

When Theo finally fell asleep, he had decided that he would go.

As you might expect, Theo was not really all that happy about meeting Alix in the middle of the night. He'd been impressed by the way she'd stood up to Grandma at the café but he still wasn't sure he liked her. After all, she'd hardly been friendly.

But after the desperate plea from his dead relatives, Theo had made up his mind and he wasn't going to let his family down just because of a few misgivings about the not-really-dead girl. So at midnight on Monday, carrying his torch and his small blue-and-green knapsack, he slipped out of Vanilla Villas and by twenty-past twelve was standing outside the Plaza cinema.

There was a late showing of a film called *Zombies from the Sands*. A few people who'd left the cinema early were milling around waiting for taxis. Theo kept close to the wall and hoped he wasn't too conspicuous. Although it was June, it was a cool night and he stamped his feet to keep warm.

Half-past twelve came and went but there was no sign of Alix. Theo wondered whether they had clocks in Deadland. If you were dead then that was it, wasn't it? Time didn't matter any longer. Why worry about being on time when you had for ever? Even if they did have clocks, he wasn't sure Alix would bother to turn up. Why should she?

By twenty-to-one Theo was beginning to hope that Alix wasn't going to show up. At least nobody would blame him for not going through with the evening's plans. But although he was there this time without any bullying from Grandma, Theo reckoned that if this evening didn't work out, she'd still want him to have another go. She'd organize another plan and sooner or later he'd have to go through with it. And let's face it, success in Grandma's scheme was his only hope of getting rid of her for good.

As one o'clock struck, Theo was still waiting. He began to think that he might have another go on his own. He hadn't any idea of what he would do but perhaps if he walked home past the Jellicon

Comestibles building, he'd be lucky and something would occur to him.

Theo had just decided to go home when he saw a ghostly figure approaching. As it wandered down the street, it went straight through a lamp-post.

What was it about ghosts? They didn't seem to care how they moved through the world. It was as if they didn't mind if people saw them. Of course, most people couldn't see them, but Theo could. And surely he wasn't the only one?

As the ghost came closer, he saw that it was Wat.

Wat smiled at Theo but said nothing.

"Where's Alix?" asked Theo.

"I think she's coming," said Wat. "Just late."

"Ah," said Theo. "What have you been up to, Wat?"

"Oh, this and that," said Wat, twisting his greasy leather apron in his hands. "I'm sorry about the fish tank, surprising you like that."

"Oh . . . that's all right, Wat."

Wat grinned with relief.

Theo couldn't help liking him. There was something so inept but well-meaning about him.

"What's that say?" said Wat, pointing to the poster for the film.

"Can't you read, Wat?" said Theo.

Wat shook his head. "I'm learning though. That's a W, isn't it?" Wat pointed to an M. "My name begins with W."

Theo began to read from the poster. "'*Zombies of the Sands* – a small seaside town is invaded when the dead come back to—'"

Then he leapt backwards in surprise as Alix's head appeared in the middle of the poster. She grinned. There seemed to be a few flies stuck to her teeth. "That was funny," she said as she pushed through the wall to join them on the pavement.

"So you think so, do you?" muttered Theo. He'd got quite a shock.

"Yeah, what a joke! The man sitting next to me was really scared."

"You mean you've been watching the film?" cried Theo.

"Yeah."

"But I've been waiting since half-past twelve!"

"Yeah, well I'm late." Alix sniffed loudly.

People started to leave the cinema. They left in twos and threes, talking about the film. Nobody took any notice of Theo, who seemed to be talking to a poster.

"Here, you can't come," said Alix to Wat.

Wat looked uncomfortable.

"Why can't he?" asked Theo. Wat looked so disappointed.

"No," said Alix. "He sets off things."

"What things?"

Wat was looking at the pavement.

"Alarms," said Alix.

Then Theo understood. So it was Wat who had set off the alarm in Jellicon's office. He looked sharply at Wat.

"I don't mean to, really I don't. . ." said Wat. "It just sort of happens. . ."

"Yeah, but if you come along and the alarm goes off, it'll be Theo that gets eaten by the big dog."

"What big dog?" asked Theo.

"Didn't you know? The guard patrols the factory with a big dog. A Doby-something."

"A Doberman," gasped Theo. He was beginning to wish he hadn't come after all and was safely back home in bed.

They set off through the streets towards Jellicon Comestibles, Theo keeping to the shadows. After ten minutes, Theo could see the large brick building at the end of the street.

"You must go now, Wat," said Alix.

"Oh, all right," moaned Wat and shambled off. Theo watched as he walked through a car, setting off the alarm, the lights flashing. Wat turned and waved to them before walking on.

"See what I mean?" said Alix.

They approached the main entrance of the Jellicon Comestibles building. Through the glass doors Theo could see the security guard sitting behind the desk, reading a magazine.

"We're not going to walk straight in, are we?" he said.

Alix snorted with laughter. "You an idiot? We've got to turn the alarm off first."

"How are we going to do that?"

"We're not. I'm going to do it," said Alix.

"But how?"

"Easy. The guard's got a sort of key that goes in a slot at the desk. Then he punches in some numbers. I watched him last night."

"But surely you won't be able to do that. How will you hold the key? Won't your hand just go straight through?"

"Nah. I'll be able to do it. I knocked your drink over, remember." Alix grinned. "You stay here, where the guard can't see you. It won't take a minute."

She set off across the road. When she reached the glass doors she walked through. Theo saw that she had to push against the glass a little. As she passed through, there was the same slight sucking noise that he'd heard in the café. Walking through something was definitely different for her. It took some effort. The other ghosts just went through as if nothing was there.

The security man glanced up briefly and then went on reading his magazine. He obviously couldn't see Alix. There was no sign of the dog.

Alix crouched by the desk and started to pull the chain that was clipped to the man's belt. The alarm key was in his pocket. Alix pulled slowly and carefully so that he didn't notice. When the man shifted in his chair, she gave a swift tug and out fell the keys. There was a whole bunch of them. Theo, watching from the shadows across the street, was amazed that the man didn't notice. But he was completely absorbed in his magazine.

Keeping an eye on the guard, Alix lifted the alarm key and tried to fit it into the slot at the desk. The weight of the other keys made it difficult for her and Theo could see that she was struggling. Worse still, however hard she tried, the chain wouldn't reach. She gave up and gently let go of the keys. The man was sitting too far away.

From across the street, Theo watched as Alix clenched her fists in frustration. She had to get the guard closer to the desk. She had to find a way of getting him to move. Theo began to wonder if she'd manage it. He wished there was something he could do but he was powerless to help her.

Alix started making faces at the guard. He went on reading. Then she moved to one side and started blowing on the man's neck. She blew quite hard.

The man shifted in his chair and then started rubbing the back of his neck. He seemed uncomfortable. Theo realized that the man could feel Alix's breath on his neck and that he couldn't understand where the draught was coming from. The man got up and crossed to the door. As he checked to see that the door was properly closed, he noticed that his bunch of keys was hanging at his side. He shrugged, put them back in his pocket, then went back to his chair. Theo sighed. Now Alix would have to start all over again.

But as the guard was about to sit down, Alix gave the chair a gentle shove. The guard flopped down in the chair, without appearing to notice anything odd, and Theo was relieved to see that it was now a little closer to the desk. As soon as the man was settled and safely reading his magazine, Alix removed the keys from his pocket for the second time. This time the chain reached and she managed to push the alarm key into its slot in the control panel. Quickly she began to punch in the numbers.

At that moment, Theo noticed movement in the corridor behind the desk. A second security guard was approaching. With him was a large dog on a leash. As they came towards the desk, the dog pricked up its ears. Suddenly it lurched forwards, jerking the leash from the guard's grip. Its teeth bared, it made straight for Alix.

Alix must have heard the dog coming. She glanced up, flinching as she realized that the dog could see her. Swiftly she tugged the alarm key from its slot and then backed hurriedly away, turning the instant she reached the door so as to pass through the glass.

She only just made it. The dog, snapping at her heels, slammed into the door behind her. Theo was sure he saw the glass wobble and for a moment he thought the dog was going to pass through too. But it slid downwards, its nose and the soft folds around its mouth flattened against the pane. With a look of surprise, it slumped into a heap on the floor.

Theo saw the security men exchange surprised looks. The man at the desk, who had leapt from his chair, noticed that his keys were again hanging by his side. He seemed a bit puzzled but put them straight back in his pocket. The behaviour of the dog was far more interesting.

"That was close," said Theo when Alix joined him at the corner of the street. "The dog nearly got you."

"Nah, it didn't. No problem," said Alix, sounding casual about the whole thing, though Theo could see she was shaken.

"But it saw you. The dog saw you!"

"So what? It happens sometimes."

"But it might have bitten you."

"No, it wouldn't. It would just have gone through. Like that." Alix swept her hand through a lamp-post.

"Are you sure?" Theo thought she looked bewildered. He was almost certain the dog had given her a big fright.

"*Of course I'm sure!*" yelled Alix.

"OK, OK." Theo thought he'd better change the subject. "Did you switch off the alarm?"

"Yeah, what d'you think I was doing?" said Alix.

"Well done," said Theo, trying to make things better. "We can get on with it then." He wanted to get the job over with now. It was taking too long. The incident with the dog had unsettled him.

"OK, this way," said Alix. She set off down a side street.

"Why are we going down here?" asked Theo.

"We've got to get up on the roof. We can get into the factory through a door on the roof. The building at the end of this street connects with Jellicon."

"But won't the door be locked?"

"It was open yesterday."

They walked along the street until it narrowed to a dimly lit passageway. Alix led the way to where there was a metal spiral staircase. It was the fire escape for the building behind Jellicon's. The building was empty, closed for a refit. Workmen had been cleaning the outside stonework and the whole of one side was enclosed in scaffolding.

Alix raced off up the staircase. She almost seemed to be able to fly up it. Theo did his best to keep up. He found it tough going and had to pause for breath.

"Hang on!" he gasped.

"Can't you go any faster? Time's getting on," said Alix.

"I know," panted Theo, reaching the top, "but I can't go as fast as you." Theo looked across at the Jellicon factory. "How are we going to get across?"

"The scaffolding at the corner," said Alix.

"Not jump?" Theo didn't like heights.

"No, there are some planks."

It sounded dangerous. "Oh, great!" he muttered to himself. "So now I've got to walk a plank 30 metres above the ground." Then, like a lightning bolt, a thought struck him. Maybe the ghosts were trying to get him killed? Perhaps that was exactly what his grandma wanted! She wanted him with her in Deadland. Then she'd be able to control him *for ever*. There'd be no escape. He'd have to do everything she wanted. Theo could hardly bear to think about it. Surely not? Surely his grandma couldn't really be planning *that*?

"Hey, hurry up!" said Alix. She was standing at the corner of the roof, where the building and the Jellicon factory came closest to each other.

"Sorry," said Theo, doing his best to put thoughts of his grandma out of his head. He needed all his wits about him.

"This is where we can cross," said Alix.

Theo gulped. It was worse than he had expected. There was a mass of scaffold poles and then just two planks across the gap. It was a long way down to the street.

"Come on, it's easy," said Alix. She was standing on the planks, over the gap.

"Oh, it's all right for you," said Theo. "You're already dead. You won't die if you fall."

For a second or two, Alix stood silently, screwing her fists in rage. "*I am not dead!*" she spat and then she turned and stomped across the planks.

Theo knew at once what was going to happen next. He saw it coming but he could do nothing about it. As if in slow motion, he saw Alix lose her footing. Her boots lost their grip, she slipped off the planks and tumbled into the air.

16

As she began to fall, Alix flung out her hands, frantically trying to grab the edge of a plank. With a desperate effort, she just managed to grip the slippery wood. Clinging on by her fingertips, she swayed back and forth beneath the plank, and for a sickening moment Theo thought she was still going to fall. At last the plank steadied and Alix tried to pull herself up, to climb back on top, but she couldn't manage it.

"Hang on!" called Theo.

"*What do you think I'm doing?*" screamed Alix.

Theo tried not to think about the danger. He just knew he must do something. Crouching down, he edged slowly across the planks towards Alix.

As soon as he was close enough, Theo grabbed hold of Alix's wrists. She was so cold to touch that the shock nearly made him let go. He hoped he had enough strength to pull her up. But he needn't have worried. The moment he started to take her weight he found, to his surprise, that she hardly weighed anything at all. A gentle pull and she was safely back on the roof of the Jellicon building.

"I'm sorry about just now," said Theo. "I know you're not like the others."

Alix said nothing. She had sat down in a huddle, her arms wrapped about her knees.

Theo wondered what would have happened if Alix had lost her grip and fallen the 30 metres to the hard pavement below. After all, she wasn't dead. Could she die? But she wasn't properly alive either. Judging by the way she walked through walls, perhaps she would have sunk through the pavement, gradually slowing to a stop deep beneath the earth. But then what would have happened? Would she have been able to get back out again? Or would she have remained trapped, buried in the soil, neither dead nor alive? Theo shuddered to think of it.

"Are you all right?" he asked. He put a hand on her shoulder.

"Get off!" she said, shaking him off roughly. "Course I'm all right."

She seemed to be herself again, though Theo wasn't sure. He could only guess at her feelings. He thought she was hiding something, though he'd no idea what. He couldn't make her out at all.

Alix got to her feet and started off across the roof.

"Where are you going? Hey, Alix, come back," called Theo but the girl had disappeared. "Oh, great! Grandma, you're a genius. Deadland's most accomplished mastermind. You really know how to organize things. What sort of help is this? Eh? The girl's hopeless!" Theo kicked the brick parapet at the edge of the roof. "Aarrggh! How did I get into this mess?"

He set off in the direction Alix had taken, looking around the rooftop. Where had she got to?

Alix appeared briefly from behind a chimney, dashed across the roof and disappeared again behind more brickwork. Theo hurried after her.

"Alix, listen. I'm sorry," he called. He approached carefully, hoping she would stay put and not run off again.

It was beginning to get light. The rooftops were getting clearer by the minute. It would soon be morning. They couldn't keep running about like this. Theo stepped up to where he thought Alix was hiding.

"Please, Alix. I need your help. I think we need to do this together." He'd got a feeling this was it. He didn't know why but he felt sure this was what his grandma had wanted all along. She didn't simply want Pete to get back his bottom. There was some reason why he and Alix should work together. It seemed crazy, but he thought he'd better go along with it. "Alix, please."

Alix moved slowly out from her hiding place.

"All right," she said. "But shut up about what happened back there." She stared intently at Theo for a moment, then waved at him to follow. "Come on, then."

She led the way across the roof to the glazed door, where they were going to enter the jam factory. Theo tried the handle.

"It's locked. I thought you said it would be open." He tried to keep his voice even.

"It was, yesterday," said Alix. "Somebody must have shut it."

Now how were they to get in? Theo studied the door. It looked strong and he didn't think it could be forced from the outside. The glass was reinforced with wire mesh so breaking that would be no good. Theo peered through. He could see that there was a push bar on the inside, for emergencies. That seemed to be their only chance, as long as Alix had enough strength to operate it.

"Can you get through the door?" he asked Alix. He wondered if she'd been affected by nearly falling off the planks.

"Yeah, I expect so," said Alix. Theo was relieved that she seemed to be cheering up. "Here goes. . ." She placed her hands on the glass, pushing slightly, and eased her way through the door.

"See that metal bar? If you can push that up the door will open," explained Theo.

Alix nodded. She tried pushing the bar. It wouldn't budge. She hadn't enough strength.

"Wait a moment," said Theo.

He looked about for inspiration. There must be some way they could open the door.

Nearby was a stack of bits and pieces that some workmen had left behind. Theo went to investigate. There were empty paint tins and a few pieces of metal. Theo found what he was looking for, a long thin strip of steel, a bit like a ruler. He tested it to see that it wouldn't bend too easily. Then he took it back to the doorway.

He knelt down and tried to push the metal strip

through the narrow gap between the bottom edge of the door and its frame. It was a tight fit but eventually he managed to slide it through to Alix on the other side. When she'd got hold of the metal, Theo showed her what to do by moving his arms about and miming how to use the strip as a lever. She soon got the idea. The metal was heavy for her but she managed to wedge one end under the bar on the door. Using all her strength, she forced the metal strip upwards. Theo could see how hard it was for her. Then all of a sudden the bar moved and the door sprung open.

"Brilliant!" cried Theo.

Alix grinned and flopped down, exhausted. Theo thought he saw a hint of pink in her face, although it might have been a trick of the early morning light.

"OK, come on," said Alix, getting up a few minutes later. She'd hardly recovered and Theo went to give her a hand but she pushed him away.

They went down a short flight of steps and then decended a spiral staircase on to a metal walkway inside the jam factory. Theo took a torch from his knapsack but they didn't really need it; there was just enough light from the windows for them to see their way. Below them, the mass of machinery was dimly lit by a few electric lights. All was quiet.

Alix led the way towards the offices at the other end of the building. They walked quickly, Theo trying to make as little noise as possible on the metal walkway. Alix made no noise at all.

At one point, Alix stopped and held her finger to her lips for quiet. She pointed down. Theo saw the second security guard with the Doberman walk past beneath them. He hardly dared breathe until they had passed.

They reached the offices at the far end of the building. Alix went on ahead to check that the coast was clear and to locate the door to Josiah Jellicon's office. They dodged inside, closing the door softly behind them.

The window blind was down and it was quite dark in the room. Rather than pull up the blind, Theo switched on his torch, hoping that way he wouldn't disturb the piranhas. He swept the torch beam briefly around the room, then moved forward to the fish tank. A stream of bubbles sparkled in the torchlight. Theo shone the torch around slowly, all around the bottom of the tank. He did it a second time, to make sure. Something was badly wrong.

"It's not there," whispered Theo.

"What?" said Alix, coming over.

"The bone. Pete's bottom. It's not in the fish tank."

"Are you sure?" said Alix.

"Yes, look," said Theo. For a third time he shone the torch slowly across the sand at the bottom of the fish tank. Nothing. The bone had disappeared.

17

It may be that you are one of those happy people who is always organized, everything is always where it should be and you have never lost anything in your life. But let me tell you, suddenly finding that something is not where you thought it was can be a very unsettling experience.

Theo was not the most organized person. He was quite used to losing things and going for weeks without finding them. By and large, he was not particularly bothered. But on this occasion, you won't be surprised to learn, he was pretty annoyed. If you had just risked life and limb breaking in to a place to find that the very thing you were after was no longer there then you would be pretty annoyed too.

"Oh, no!" wailed Theo. "Now what?"

"Perhaps he's hidden it," said Alix.

As the bone was obviously no longer in the fish tank, they began to search the rest of Jellicon's office. Theo switched off his torch and opened the blind at the window to give them more light. It was nearly daylight outside and that made searching a lot easier. They looked on the desk, on the shelves, in the cupboards and drawers and even in the wastepaper basket. But they didn't find Pete's bone.

"A safe!" said Theo, coming out from under the desk. "That's it. Why didn't I think of it before? He's put it in a safe!"

"A what?" said Alix.

"A safe. You know, like a cupboard with a special lock. Used for storing things that you don't want people to see . . . or steal. . . Usually they're hidden, behind a picture or something. Jellicon's bound to have a safe."

As there were only three pictures on the walls of Mr Jellicon's office, it took only a minute to look behind each one. Behind the picture of a hippopotamus there was a large brown stain on the wall. Behind the picture of Tower Bridge in the rain there was a large squashed spider. And behind the picture of a small man with a very large moustache (a "Mr Lloyd

Teddington" according to the nameplate on the frame), there was the door to a safe. This picture had an ornate gold-leaf frame that was extremely heavy and Alix had to help Theo lift it off the wall.

It's one thing to find a safe – that's not too difficult if you know the sort of places to look – but it's altogether a different problem getting inside. The whole point about safes is that they are "safe". You're not meant to be able to open them unless you own them.

However, Theo and Alix had a few advantages over the rest of us. Afterwards it occurred to Theo that he might have a great future ahead of him, although a criminal one, if he were to team up with Alix and break into safes. Except that it wasn't necessary for them to "break into" this safe. They didn't need drills or explosives. They simply opened the door.

It was one of those safes that has a dial and numbers. You twiddled the dial in different directions until you reached the different numbers. All you needed then was the right combination and – Bob's your uncle – you could open the door. Of course, if you didn't know the numbers then you couldn't open the door. Unless, that is, you had someone like Alix to help you.

Theo explained to Alix how the safe worked and then she stuck her hands through to the mechanism. Theo began to twiddle the dial. Each time Alix felt the wheel "click" at the right number, she nodded and then Theo turned the wheel back and tried for the next number. In a few moments there was a final "click" and the door swung open.

The inside was stuffed full of things.

Theo pulled out a whole lot of bits of paper, an old watch and a cracked teapot before he found Pete's pelvis.

"At last!" said Theo, as he pulled out the bone and held it up to show Alix. It was lighter than he'd expected and he handled it gingerly, afraid of dropping it. It wouldn't do to break it. He put it safely into his knapsack.

"Hey, look at that!" cried Alix, pointing to a stuffed toy that was sitting towards the back of the safe.

"Hey, it's a teddy bear!" exclaimed Theo. "Fancy Jellicon having a teddy bear in his safe!"

They grinned at each other.

At that moment they heard voices from the other side of the office door. Then there was the sound of a vacuum cleaner.

"Blimey! The cleaners are here already," said Theo.

He began stuffing the things back into the safe. "What time is it?"

"It's ten past six," said Alix, looking at the clock on the wall.

"Can you have a look and see if the cleaners are coming this way?"

Alix stuck her head through the door.

"You'd better hide," she said. "They look as though they're going to do this room next."

"Drat," muttered Theo. Quickly he closed the safe. Alix helped him put the picture back on its nail and then, grabbing his knapsack, Theo darted into a tall cupboard. It was the only place he could see to hide.

As he crouched inside the cupboard, Theo heard the office door open. There was a narrow gap in the cupboard door through which he could just see two women walk into the room.

"Here, this doesn't need much doing, does it?" said one, who wore a blue ribbon in her hair. She held the handle of a vacuum cleaner.

"No, a quick dust'll be enough," said the other, coughing loudly into her duster. "Oh, and that picture's not straight."

"Ah, poor Mr Teddington," said the woman with the ribbon as she straightened the picture. "Fancy

110

him getting lost in the Amazon jungle like that."

"Yes, they reckon he was eaten by piranhas," said her partner, who was dusting the desk.

"Funny that. Mr Jellicon liking piranhas and all."

"He's very fond of those fish. He doesn't feed them any old rubbish."

"Treats them better than his staff, then!"

The women giggled.

"It's true. He gets fresh fruit sent from London specially."

"He doesn't!"

"Yes he does. They only eat fruit. Think of that, vegetarian piranhas!"

Theo, listening inside the cupboard, ground his teeth in dismay. Could it be true? Vegetarian piranhas? If it was, then Jellicon had tricked him and he could have taken the bone easily the first time.

The woman with the ribbon started the vacuum cleaner and began cleaning around the desk.

Theo wondered how long he'd have to stay hidden. It was cramped inside the cupboard. Then suddenly someone touched his arm and he jumped, hitting the side of the cupboard with a clang. It was lucky the vacuum cleaner was so noisy or the women would surely have heard. Alix had joined him.

"You'll have to stay here for the moment," she said.

"But I can't stay here all day!" gasped Theo.

"Well the building's full of people now. You won't get out without being spotted. Perhaps when the machinery's going and everybody's busy, you won't attract attention and we can slip back on to the roof. I'll keep an eye on things and let you know." She disappeared again.

What a disaster, thought Theo.

But there was worse to come.

"Good morning, ladies," said a voice that Theo recognized instantly. It was Josiah Jellicon.

"Good morning, Mr Jellicon. You're here early today," said the cleaners.

"Yes, lots to do today," said Jellicon. "Thank you ladies, that will do for now."

Peeping through the crack in the door, Theo saw Jellicon hurry the cleaning women out, closing the door behind them.

Now, you might think that Theo was in a bad situation but that all he had to do was sit tight and wait for an opportunity to escape. Well, let me give you a word of advice. If ever you decide to do something and you don't want to get caught doing it, make sure that you don't leave any telltale signs lying about.

112

That sort of carelessness can get you into big trouble.

For a few minutes Theo listened to Jellicon humming to himself and moving around the office.

Then something happened that made Theo's heart sink into his boots.

Josiah Jellicon spoke clearly.

"All right, Theo Slugg, you can come out now."

18

There was nothing for it. Theo knew he was beaten. He pushed open the cupboard door and stepped into the room.

Josiah Jellicon was perched on the edge of his desk. In one hand he held Theo's torch. "Theo Slugg, P4," he read from the label Theo had stuck on for a school trip. "Hmm, why *is* that name familiar? . . .Anyway, it's fortunate that you are so good at labelling your property, Mr Slugg. Especially when you are so careless as to leave it lying around."

Theo nodded, staring at the floor. He could have kicked himself. He'd put the torch down on the desk when they'd started searching the office but he'd forgotten all about it when they were opening the safe.

"You've got a nerve," went on Jellicon. "I suppose

you've broken in here after that silly bone? You're persistent, I'll give you that. I admire persistence, Slugg. But, as you will have found out, I anticipated you this time. The bone was not where you thought it would be."

With a shock of surprise Theo realized that Jellicon had no idea that he had Pete's bone in his knapsack. He would have to be careful to keep a straight face. While there was the slightest chance of him escaping he mustn't give himself away.

"Don't think you're going to get away with it though," continued Jellicon. "I can't let a demented child like you break in here just because you feel like it. I can tell you, I've a good mind to tip you straight into the jam-making machine. It's the latest model, very efficient. You'd disappear in no time. After just two minutes of mashing and boiling, you'd be raspberry jam. Everybody's favourite. Nobody would ever know."

The thought of becoming raspberry jam horrified Theo. He considered making a dash for the window. Then he remembered he was two floors up.

"But I'm not a cruel man," continued Jellicon. "I shall hand you over to the proper authorities. But just now, it's inconvenient – there's a government health inspector arriving shortly and you and the police would be something of an embarrassment – so for the time being you'll just have to get back into your hiding place."

Jellicon opened the cupboard door. Theo had no choice but to climb inside.

"And don't think of escaping," said Jellicon, as he closed the door on Theo. "I shall have the key in my pocket, so you might as well settle down and make yourself comfortable. If you've been up half the night, you might like to have a sleep. You'll have a few hours to wait until I can call the police."

Theo heard the key turn in the lock. Peering through the crack in the door he could just see Jellicon at his desk, shifting through some papers. At one point Jellicon went across to the picture of Mr Teddington. For a nasty moment, Theo thought that he was going to open the safe but then, to Theo's relief, Jellicon seemed to change his mind and went back to the desk. He picked up the phone.

"Ah, Braithwaite. This is Jellicon. There's been a small change of plan. Chandler tells me that the inspector will turn up about ten. Yes, Chandler is my man at the board office. So can we have the raspberries in for nine-thirty? Good. Yes, good man.

The usual, of course. Thanks, goodbye."

Jellicon put down the telephone, collected a few papers and came over to the cupboard.

"Remember Slugg, one squeak out of you and you're boiled and bottled," he snarled, his voice so menacing that it sent shivers down Theo's spine. Theo heard the door of the office open and close as Jellicon went out.

Sitting squashed up at the bottom of the cupboard, Theo puzzled over what to do. He certainly didn't intend to just wait there until Jellicon handed him over to the police. He wondered where Alix had disappeared to. The girl was hopeless. If she had been there she might have managed to get the key off Jellicon and unlock the door.

It was warm and dark in the cupboard. Theo yawned. As you would expect, after being up all night, he was more than a little tired. He tried hard to keep his eyes open but gradually his eyelids drooped. It wasn't very long before he began to doze and finally he fell fast asleep.

Theo woke with a start. For a moment he didn't know where he was.

"Ohhh!" he groaned. He ached all over. Cupboards

are not the most comfortable places to sleep. He peered at his watch, trying to make out the time in the dim light. It was twenty to eleven. He must have been asleep for hours.

By now the health inspector would have arrived and Jellicon was probably busy showing him around the factory. It would be a good time to try and escape.

He stood up and considered the matter. Perhaps, if he pressed hard enough, he'd be able to force the door, buckling and breaking the lock. Theo put both hands on the door and pushed. Nothing happened. He braced himself against the sides and tried again. Still nothing happened.

The best way to break open a locked door is to throw your weight against it. What is perfectly strong and secure under gradual pressure will often give way when a sudden force is applied. But Theo couldn't rush at the door. There wasn't enough room. Instead he squashed himself flat against the back wall of the cupboard, took a deep breath and then flung himself at the door with all the strength he could muster.

Theo thought he saw the door give, just a tiny bit. Encouraged by this, he took another deep breath, and had another go.

With an almighty crash, the cupboard fell over.

As luck would have it, the fall broke the lock on the cupboard door. Unfortunately, the cupboard landed face down, so Theo was still stuck inside. He was a bit stunned and bruised but otherwise all right. Holding on to the inside, he started to rock back and forth in the hope of rolling the cupboard on to its side.

After a lot of effort, Theo finally managed it. The cupboard tottered over and the door fell open.

A face peered in through the opening.

"Good gracious, Mr Windrush! What *are* you doing in there?"

It was Miss Moulder, the lady from the reception desk.

19

Theo was about to answer but he only got as far as opening his mouth. At that instant the picture of Mr Lloyd Teddington fell off the wall. The rather thin nail, that had supported the picture for several years, had finally bent and the picture slipped off. As it plunged towards the floor, it hit the back of Miss Moulder's head with such a thwack that it knocked her out cold.

Theo struggled to get out of the cupboard. To do this, he had to shift both Miss Moulder and Mr Teddington. It took him some considerable effort. As I've already mentioned, Mr Teddington, or at least his frame, was not light. Miss Moulder was no feather-weight either. Gasping with the exertion, Theo at last managed to extract himself and stood up.

"Phew!" he puffed.

He grabbed his torch and stuffed it into the front pocket of his knapsack where it wouldn't bash against Pete's bone. Then he made sure that the bag was safely strapped to his back before he stepped lightly to the door and peeped out.

All was clear.

Theo decided that he couldn't go down the stairs to the main door. There was bound to be a man at the desk. He'd have to go back through the factory.

He was just about to hurry down the corridor when he nearly tripped over Alix, who was sitting on the floor behind Miss Moulder's desk. She had on some little headphones and was listening to music.

"Urr urrr, ba ba ba urr murrrr!" groaned Alix, rocking along with the noise.

"Hey!" cried Theo. Alix was so involved with the music that she took no notice. He tugged at her sleeve. She looked up.

"What?" she shouted.

Theo pulled off the headphones. "What are you doing here?" he hissed.

"What do you think I'm doing?"

"You mean, while I've been stuck in there, you've been listening to music?"

"You were asleep," said Alix. "I saw you."

"Well, why didn't you wake me?"

"I thought I'd wait a bit," grumbled Alix. "Until they'd gone home."

"But that wouldn't have been for ages!" groaned Theo. "I've got to get out of here *now*. Are you coming?"

But Alix wasn't listening. She'd put the headphones back on.

"Ru ru ru, ba ba!" she sang.

"Are you coming?" repeated Theo, crossly.

"*What?*" shouted Alix.

"Hopeless!" muttered Theo. He tugged at the headphones. "*I've got to go!*" he cried.

"All right, all right! I can hear you," said Alix. She scrambled up, shoving the headphones and player back on the desk where she'd found them.

They set off along the corridor towards the factory, keeping a sharp lookout. Alix went a little way ahead so that they didn't run into anyone unexpectedly. But that part of the building was deserted. Everybody seemed to be involved in the health inspector's visit. So far, so good, thought Theo.

When they reached the factory, there were lots of people about and Theo had to be more careful. But luckily all the activity was on the floor below. And on their level there were plenty of things to hide behind if Theo needed to get out of sight quickly.

As he followed Alix along the walkway, Theo glanced around. The factory was a huge space, full of all sorts of machinery. There were machines for chopping, crushing and mashing. Huge hoppers fed ingredients on to conveyor belts, which in turn led to enormous vats where the mixture was stirred and boiled. On hundreds of shelves, thousands of jars were stacked, ready for filling, labelling and boxing.

Theo wondered where his father was. He couldn't see him or anything that looked like a raspberry pip machine. Then he spotted Jellicon. With him was a man with a clipboard: the health inspector.

Alix had seen them too. She stopped by some boxes of chutney and waited for Theo.

"Stay here until they look the other way," she said.

Theo nodded. In order to reach the spiral staircase and the exit on to the roof, they had to pass in front of where Jellicon was walking with the inspector. If Theo was to avoid being spotted he'd have to pick the right moment.

Jellicon was showing the health inspector the conveyor belts that carried the fruit for the jam. That day it was raspberries; raspberries that Theo knew had been brought in specially. The inspector kept writing things down on his clipboard. Theo could see that Jellicon was agitated, wanting to see what the inspector was writing. With them were several other people from the factory. Everybody had on white coats and hats. The inspector started looking closely at a conveyor belt.

"OK, let's go!" cried Alix and she set off towards the staircase.

As Theo was about to follow, Jellicon suddenly glanced his way. Theo pulled back quickly, hoping that he hadn't been seen.

When you have a knapsack on your back, it is very easy to forget it is there. It's only when you've turned round and knocked over a valuable vase or something that you remember. By which time the damage is done.

And another thing, you should always be careful when you are near machinery that you don't have any loose clothing. As you might guess, this is because loose things can become caught in machinery, with unpleasant consequences.

Unfortunately, as Theo backed away from the railing, he forgot that he was wearing his knapsack.

One of the straps from the knapsack became

caught on part of a sort of crane. The crane wasn't moving but as Theo stumbled backwards he also happened to knock a lever which started the thing going. He was abruptly swept upwards. Dangling from the crane, he tried desperately to grab hold of something to try and stop himself being carried higher. The nearest thing was a huge container, almost as big as a bus, covered by a tarpaulin.

The crane juddered and strained as Theo hung upside down, clinging for dear life to the edge of the container. Something had to give and fortunately for Theo, it wasn't him but the straps of his knapsack. They ripped apart and Theo tumbled into the container, leaving the knapsack still caught on the crane. He landed on the tarpaulin but wasn't in the least hurt as whatever was underneath was soft and bouncy. It was as if he had fallen on to a huge mattress.

Theo was immediately aware of a very strong smell of the sea. He pulled back a loose edge of the cover and wasn't the least surprised to find that he'd landed in a great tub full of seaweed. So Jellicon did use it!

I should point out that seaweed is very good stuff. It has a lot of uses and is rich in good things like minerals. It is not rubbish. Far from it. Josiah Jellicon used it because it was cheaper than the fruit and vegetables that were supposed to go into his jams and chutneys. Nothing wrong with that, you might say. But Jellicon claimed that only the finest ingredients went into his products. The finest seaweed? That's OK by me, you might argue. But – and this is the bad bit – the labels said that there was lots of fruit in his jams when in fact, there was hardly any. And the seaweed wasn't mentioned at all.

Theo was now stuck in the seaweed container, which had sides that were far too high for him to reach the rim. The tarpaulin wasn't any help as it had come loose when he had fallen in. He tried jumping up and down to see if he could reach the edge that way. Perhaps if he could just grab it with his hands he'd be able to climb out.

The seaweed was quite bouncy and, rather as on a trampoline, with every jump Theo managed to get a little bit higher. After five attempts, Theo managed to catch hold of the rim. He lifted up his right leg and was just putting his foot on to the edge when the container began to tip.

Theo slipped and slid but there was nothing he could do. The container tipped right over and he was thrown out, along with fifteen tonnes of seaweed, straight on to the conveyor belt of raspberries.

The belt was moving quite fast. Theo struggled desperately, trying to crawl from under the mixture of seaweed and raspberries. He had to get off quickly, before he was thrown into a vat and boiled and churned into raspberry jam.

At last Theo surfaced. Several people beside the conveyor belt recoiled in horror, thinking that he was some kind of strange sea monster. Clearing bits of smelly seaweed from his face, he turned round to find that he was being carried straight towards Josiah Jellicon and the health inspector. Jellicon's eyes bulged wide at the sight of Theo and the health inspector's jaw dropped in astonishment.

"*Stop this machine at once!*" barked the health inspector. A man in a white coat ran to the switch. The conveyor belt shuddered to a halt and Theo stopped right beside the inspector.

"Mr Jellicon, that looks to me like a small boy. Do you usually put small boys into your raspberry jam?" asked the inspector sternly.

"Ah. Is that a small boy?" mumbled Jellicon, purple with rage. "Are you sure? Isn't it a very large raspberry. . .?"

The inspector ignored him. He was consulting his clipboard.

"And seaweed doesn't seem to be in your list of usual ingredients. I think I had better have a private word with you in your office, Mr Jellicon, please."

"Yes. Yes. Of course," muttered Jellicon. He glowered at Theo and then turned to lead the way to his office, the inspector marching beside him. The other members of the group followed sheepishly behind.

Theo struggled off the conveyor belt, brushing the bits of seaweed from his shoulders. The factory workers shrunk back, still unsure of what to make of him. Theo realized he must look a strange sight with bits of seaweed and raspberry juice all over him. But he'd no time to worry about that. With Jellicon occupied explaining things to the health inspector, it would be a good moment to make his escape. But first he must try and find his knapsack. He couldn't leave without Pete's bone.

Theo started to make his way back towards the crane, looking left and right in the hope of finding his bag. The factory workers, anxious not to get into trouble, went back to their work. They were all too busy to take much notice of him. Then Theo saw Alix.

"There you are! Good, come quickly," she said. She

looked very worried. "I tried to hold on to it, really I did!"

Theo ran after her as she led the way to a machine at the back of the factory where his dad was busy at the controls. The machine was the one that made raspberry pips. His dad looked up.

"Theo, what on earth are you doing here?"

"Hello Dad," said Theo. "I. . . I. . . I'm doing research for a school project."

"Oh, are you?" said Mr Slugg. "It looks messy. . ."

Alix was frantically waving her arms about, pointing to the machine which started making loud crunching and grinding noises.

"Oh! Oh! What's happening?" yelled Theo's dad in panic. He started pulling on levers and pushing buttons as fast as he could.

There was a spluttering and a sound like gunfire and then suddenly something blue and green shot out of the top of the machine. It spun in the air and then flopped on to the ground at Theo's feet. It was the remains of his knapsack.

"*Oh, NO!*" wailed Theo. He picked up the ripped and shredded bag. There was no sign of Pete's bone. The bag was empty.

Theo's dad was still trying to bring the raspberry pip machine under control. It was squealing and crunching in the most alarming manner.

Theo just couldn't believe it. Pete's bone was being turned into raspberry pips and there was nothing he could do about it. And after all that effort! After all he'd been through!

"I can't think what's got into the thing!" cried Mr Slugg.

Theo thought he knew but he wasn't going to say. He couldn't have begun to explain.

His dad tried engaging the back gear and then threw the machine into reverse. There was a loud crack like a firework going off, a blinding flash of blue light and the machine shuddered to a stop.

"Thank goodness," exclaimed Mr Slugg. "Now then, what's the trouble?" He took off the protective wire cage, opened the cover and peered inside the grinding mechanism. "Hmm, what have we here?"

Theo forced himself to look. Alix peeped over his shoulder. Surely there'd be nothing left of Pete's bone?

But what Theo's dad was holding was clearly not a piece of bone. It was a mangled piece of metal. It was hardly recognizable but Theo could just make out the letters "P4". The remains of his torch.

Theo was so anxious about what had been going on in the raspberry pip machine that he hadn't noticed a figure approach. He felt a hand grip his shoulder.

"Ah, I've got you, you little criminal. You'll not get away from me this time!" It was the security guard, the one who didn't like music. "You're coming with me."

"But—" Theo started to protest.

"What's going on?" cried Theo's dad.

"Trespassing without permission!" cried the guard. "Endangering the health and safety of the public!"

"Theo's here for a school project. . ." Theo's dad began.

But the guard wasn't going to be thwarted. He knew his duty. Mr Slugg watched helplessly as the

131

man pushed Theo roughly away towards a door at the side of the factory.

Just before they reached the door, some very loud hooters began to sound throughout the factory.

"Oh drat, it's the fire alarm!" cried the security guard. He had responsibilities. Everybody had to leave the building in an orderly fashion. Safety must come first. "OK, everybody, this way!" he called, doing his best to direct people to the exits while still holding on to Theo. But in the confusion he moment-arily relaxed his grip. Theo took his chance. Darting through the throng, he made his escape.

Theo ran back into the factory; there were too many people making for the exit and he was afraid of being caught in the crowd. He dodged around the machinery and headed for the far end of the building. That way, if he couldn't find an exit at ground level, he'd be able to get back on to the roof.

The building was almost deserted, the last few workers hurrying to the exits. Theo wondered where the fire was. There was no sign of any smoke.

Then, a minute later, the hooters were switched off. It was a false alarm. Theo would have to hurry now, before the factory began to fill with people again.

Passing beneath the crane that had caused him so

much trouble, Theo heard footsteps. He ducked behind some packing cases, crouching down so as not to be seen. The footsteps came closer. Peeping from his hiding place, Theo saw that it was the security guard. The man stopped a few metres away and looked about. Theo held his breath.

"I'll get you, you little villain!" cried the guard, setting off at a run back towards the jam vats.

"Phew, that was close," muttered Theo, with a sigh of relief.

He was just getting up when his right hand touched something hard on the box beside him. He glanced down and then nearly cried out in surprise. It was Pete's pelvis! It must have fallen from the crane when his knapsack had been ripped from his back. It seemed to be in one piece. He could hardly believe his luck.

Holding the bone tightly, Theo set off again. He was nearly at the end of the building and saw a doorway ahead. He could escape.

As he ran towards the door, he saw Alix standing nearby. Wat Kemp was with her and they were enjoying watching the mayhem.

"Thanks," cried Theo, waving as he raced past. "Thanks Wat." He was pretty sure that it had been

Wat who had set off the fire alarms. They waved back, Wat grinning broadly.

Then just as Theo reached the door, a man in uniform dashed in carrying a hose. The fire brigade had arrived.

"Where's the fire?" called the fireman.

"Down there!" shouted Theo, pointing to the jam vats.

"Thanks!" cried the fireman, and switching on his hose he rushed forward, spraying water everywhere.

Theo raced outside.

The street was in uproar. Everywhere there were firemen running about, carrying hoses which lay in great coils across the roadway. Keeping a tight grip on Pete's bone, Theo slowed his pace and stepped carefully through the mayhem.

He reached the corner of the street where two firemen where just attaching a hose to a hydrant.

"That's it, Bill! On with it, then!" cried one, who had a white helmet.

"Ooops, boss, it's gonna—" shouted the other, and then the hose burst off the hydrant and an enormous spout of water gushed out across the pavement. It hit Theo bang in the middle of his back and the force of the water knocked him clean off his feet. Instinctively he threw out his hands to save himself, letting go of Pete's bone, which was swiftly carried away by the water. Theo struggled desperately to catch hold of the bone before it was swept into the gutter. But he stumbled on the edge of the pavement and it slipped through his fingers. Completely helpless, Theo watched in horror as the bone was washed into the drain and disappeared.

If you've got an unpleasant thing to do, something there is absolutely no getting out of, then it is generally best to get on with it. Putting it off will only make it worse.

Theo put off going to see his grandma as long as possible. He couldn't face telling her that he'd had Pete's bone in his hands, that he'd come so close . . . and then lost it . . . and that now it was gone for ever.

But he knew he had no option. There was nothing for it. So eventually, late in the evening of the following day, he reluctantly got up off his bed and pressed button B.

The lift started to go downwards and then stopped with a bump at the basement. The doors slowly opened.

"Hello there," said Mr Windrush. He was sweeping carefully around the huge washing machine.

Theo, who had been expecting to go straight on down to Deadland, was at a bit of a loss.

"Er . . . hello Mr Windrush. . . Is that interesting dust?"

"Oh yes," said Mr Windrush, who was lovingly brushing dust into his dustpan. He held up the pan reverently, looking at the dust with wide-eyed admiration, as if it had magical powers. "This dust was not here yesterday. Imagine that! But I can tell it is old. It must have come from a different dimension – perhaps even a different world than ours."

Theo looked at the dust. "Do you really think so?" he said. Theo thought that probably somebody had actually used the washing machine for the first time in years and the dust had been shaken out from inside.

"Oh yes," said Mr Windrush. "You see those stringy bits?" He pointed to some green threads that were the same colour as a shirt that Theo had once had. "Well, I'm almost certain those are from the eleventh dimension."

"Really?" said Theo, trying to keep a straight face. Was Mr Windrush now on a different planet altogether?

"Yes," said Mr Windrush, seriously. "But oh! I'm so sorry – I'm stopping you from doing what you came down here for. And I should get on. I have so much to do." He went back to his brushing.

Theo stood there, looking completely baffled. What should he do?

Mr Windrush looked up. "Just press the button again," he said, waving his brush towards the lift.

Theo, puzzled by Mr Windrush's strange words, shrugged and got back into the lift. He pressed B again. The doors closed and then, to Theo's enormous surprise, the lift started travelling downwards.

After a few minutes the lift stopped. But instead of the doors opening, they stayed tight shut.

"Oh, now what?" muttered Theo, slamming his fists against the door in frustration. As he did so, his arms sank through the door as if nothing was there. Theo lost his balance and tumbled into the nothingness of Deadland.

22

"Ah, we've been expecting you," croaked a voice from the darkness, close to Theo's ear. After plunging through the door-that-wasn't-a-door, Theo had fallen flat on his face. He picked himself up and saw a toad. There were more toads sitting nearby. Were they the same toads as before, wondered Theo, the same ones that had sung to him in the lift? He was almost sure of it.

"Please don't –" he began. The last thing he wanted was singing.

"It's all right," muttered the toad, crossly. "We're not going to sing. Not for you, anyway. We're professionals. We like an appreciative audience. And besides, we've instructions to take you directly there. Come on."

Directly where? thought Theo, as he followed the toads. That sounded sinister. The toads had been waiting for him to arrive. Why? What had his grandma got planned now?

"Ow! Look where you're treading!" croaked a toad.

"Sorry!" said Theo. He'd better watch where he was putting his feet. But that was odd, he thought, how could he hurt a phantom toad, or a ghost or, for that matter, *anything* that was dead? Then he had a sudden horrible thought, a thought that sent a chill down through his body, turning his stomach to ice and his legs to jelly. Perhaps. . . Perhaps . . . *he* was *dead*!

But if he *was* dead, when had it happened? He hadn't noticed it. But then perhaps you didn't. Perhaps it just happened. He wondered if he should ask the toads. Surely they would know. But they were hopping ahead so fast that he didn't feel he could ask. He had to hurry to keep up and got quite warm doing so, despite the chilly atmosphere.

A few lights began to appear, single bulbs that didn't seem to be attached to anything. There were no fittings or ceiling above them that Theo could see. Soon he saw more lights, arranged in decorative rows, and just the hint of some walls. And then seats appeared, fixed in tiers, with pillars, curtains and even the suggestion of red carpeting on the floor. At last Theo realized that before him was an old-fashioned theatre. He wondered if it was the ghost of a theatre, if buildings became ghosts when they were knocked down and disappeared from the world of the living.

A hoard of excited little children appeared, shepherded by a number of grown-ups in grey and white uniforms. The children were all ages and were ushered into the seats as if they were going to see a performance.

Theo wanted to stop, to see what was going on, but the toads wouldn't let him. They hurried on around the theatre, to the rooms at the back.

At the back were more ghosts, all busy putting on costumes or make-up. Theo glimpsed Pete Pilkington, dressed in what looked like a new suit. He was just trying on a bowler hat and didn't notice Theo. Theo wondered glumly how he was going to break the news to him. Then he saw Grandma.

"Late as usual," she grumbled.

"I . . . I'm. . ." said Theo. He didn't know how to begin.

"Hopeless little cockroach! You couldn't manage that one simple thing, could you?"

"I tried, really I. . ." mumbled Theo.

"Oh, pull yourself together and stop gibbering. I've no time for such things."

"It was so. . . I nearly had. . . I just couldn't. . ."

"Argh!" cried Grandma. "No more pathetic excuses! You knew it was important. It's not as if you weren't given an invitation."

"An invitation? What invitation?" asked Theo, wondering what on earth his grandma was talking about.

"You . . . mean . . . you. . .?" stammered Grandma, looking as if she might explode. "Argh! Wat! Wat! Where is that good-for-nothing?"

Wat appeared, looking flustered. He grinned when he saw Theo.

"The invitation, Wat?" thundered Grandma.

Wat looked puzzled for a moment and then clapped his hand to his mouth. "Oh no, I forgot!" he wailed. He fished around in his pocket and eventually brought out a bit of crumpled card.

"Oh, why do I bother?" groaned Grandma, holding her head in her hands.

Then Alix ran in. "Pete's about to go on!" she yelled. "Made it, then!" she said to Theo with a grin.

Theo was still trying to work it all out. But his grandma was hurrying into the theatre.

"What invitation, Wat?" asked Theo, as they followed.

"For the performance!" said Wat, looking at Theo as if he was stupid.

Pete Pilkington was already on stage and had started to dance. He danced like a dream. He tossed the bowler hat around, making it roll across his shoulders and down the walking stick, while all the time his feet tapped out the most amazing tunes at a tremendous speed. Theo had never seen or heard anything like it.

"But he can dance!" whispered Theo to Alix.

"You an idiot? Of course he can dance!" said Alix.

"But the bone. . . Pete's bone. . . It went down the drain!" And then finally Theo realized. Pete *had* got his bone back. It had been washed down the drain and *into the sea* – exactly where Pete had said it should be. Theo had done it. He'd actually done it!

When Pete finished his act the audience went wild with delight. They clapped and shrieked and yelled for more. And Pete, who couldn't really help himself, danced some more. He hadn't enjoyed himself so much in a long while.

After his performance he came up to Theo.

"Thank you!" he cried. "Miraculous! Fabulous!

Absolutely stupendous!" and he shook Theo's hand with both of his at once, just to show he could do it.

Theo couldn't think what to say.

There were other acts besides Pete's. The toads came on next. They started to sing the dreadful "Cherry Trees".

"You still here?" said Grandma, looking round at Theo.

"I did it, Grandma!" said Theo.

"Eh?" muttered Grandma.

"I got Pete's bone."

"Hmm," said Grandma, ignoring him. "It's time you went. You can't hang around here, you know. Wat! Wat, show him the way. Go on, off you go!" She waved him away with her stick.

There was just no pleasing his grandma, thought Theo, as he followed Wat away from the theatre.

"And don't come back!" shouted Grandma after them. "I never want to see you again!"

As they walked on, Wat began to look worried.

"She didn't mean that," he said, when they were almost back at the lift. The doors had opened and Theo could see his things inside.

"I know, Wat, I know," said Theo, with a sigh. Then he waved goodbye and stepped into the lift.